Darkness . . .

Dylan leaned on the kitchen bench, staring out at the darkness, holding onto the bench as though a huge weight was pushing him from behind. There was sweat on his face, and he breathed in deep gasps, as if he were in pain and terrified.

He gave a cry: "Juniper!"

And then he covered his face with his arms, leaning forward over the running water and the swirl of blood in the sink, and he screamed.

Other Point paperbacks
you will enjoy:

The Promise
by Robert Westall

Storm Rising
by Marilyn Singer

Enter Three Witches
Kate Gilmore

The Haunting of Francis Rain
by Margaret Buffie

point

THE JUNIPER GAME

Sherryl Jordan

SCHOLASTIC INC.
New York Toronto London Auckland Sydney

No part of this publication may be reproduced in whole or in part, or stored in a retrieval system, or transmitted in any form, or by any means, electronic, mechanical, photocopying, recording, or otherwise, without written permission of the publisher. For information regarding permission, write to Scholastic Inc., 555 Broadway, New York, NY 10012.

ISBN 0-590-44729-7

12 11 10 9 8 7 6 5 4 3 2   4 5 6 7 8 9/9

Printed in the U.S.A.   01

For Kym,
who
read, re-read,
criticised, gave advice on,
and loved
The Juniper Game

My thanks to the Literary Fund of the QE 11 Arts Council, and Quality Packers, for awarding me the 1988 Choysa Bursary. Without that, *The Juniper Game* might not have been written.

My special thanks also to Linda Hansen for sharing with me her knowledge of herbs and medieval life, and for proof-reading the final manuscript.

S.J.

Contents

In the Beginning . . .

The girl worked quickly, pounding the dried roots in a mortar and pestle and pouring the crumbled remains onto a piece of clean cloth. Behind her a child cried irritably from a wooden cradle, but she ignored it. She finished the preparation, gathered it into a bundle in the cloth, and tied it securely with a leather strip. She placed it on the wide windowsill in the sunlight, then turned to her child.

An older woman came into the room. She sniffed suspiciously and surveyed the wooden trestle-table where the girl had worked. The evidence was all there: the remains of dried herbal plants, the strong, pungent smell of crushed valerian roots, and the small bundle in the sunlight.

"Ah, Mistress," the woman clucked, shaking her head, "this bodes not well for thee. If thy husband should find out . . ."

1

"He'll not know, nor care if he did," the girl replied calmly, bending her fair head over the child and kissing him. "Besides, 'tis only good I do. That drug is for ease of pain and blessed sleep. 'Tis a goodly thing, Nurse, not evil."

The nurse shook her head again and went out.

The girl smiled to herself and sat down on a stool, the baby laughing on her knee. A shaft of sunlight fell from the shuttered window onto the girl's head, shining on her smooth braided hair and lying in crimson pools in the hollows of her cheeks. She had a strange but beautiful face, oval shaped with wide, fine-boned cheeks and a slightly pointed chin. Her eyes were vivid blue and slanted upwards at the outer corners. She had an elfin look about her, a haunting beauty that, once seen, was never forgotten. Some said she wove spells with her brightness, and that a single glance from her eyes could enslave a young man's soul.

A cautious knock sounded on the heavy wood surrounding the window, and the girl looked up to see an ancient woman standing there, toothless and bent almost double with age and care. The girl got up, balanced the child on her hip, and took the bundle from the windowsill. She gave it to the old woman, smiling.

"It will help her, Good Mother," she said softly. "Put this in a bowl and pour over it boiling water, and steep it a while, and then do give it to her to drink. 'Twill ease her pain and help her sleep. And on the tooth that aches, put the pure juice squeezed

2

from fresh angelica. Trust me, Good Mother. I've tried it on myself."

The old woman bowed her head, folded her gnarled fingers about the medicine, and hobbled furtively away. As the girl watched her go, her face was troubled and sad.

She sighed and turned her luminous eyes on the child. He was reaching for a silver chalice on the table, so the girl gave it to him, holding it steady while he sniffed the contents and struggled to tip the chalice towards his mouth.

"Nay — it is wine and too strong for thee." The mother laughed, lifted the chalice to her own lips, and drained it. The wine sat in drops on her upper lip, like tiny rubies in the light, and she smiled and gazed lovingly at the silver cup. It had been her husband's wedding gift to her and was her most precious and treasured possession. It was engraved in intricate geometric patterns around the rim and halfway down and was inlaid with amethysts.

She put it down and half turned, her head tilted, as if she listened. The child tugged at her hair, chortling, and she took his hands in one of her own, held them still, and told the child to hush. Uneasily, she turned and faced the interior of the room. The painted plaster walls glimmered with shadows and lights from the window, and sunshine lay in bright patches on the worn stone floor. A straw broom stood propped against one wall, and branches and berries from herbal plants hung drying on the walls. Still, the girl looked about her uneasily, as though there was something she could not see.

Slowly, her eyes focused on a place in the air, about the height of her own head. Alarmed, she made the sign of the cross on her breast and pulled her child to her tightly. He started to whimper, and she closed her hand over his mouth. She backed away, breathing prayers, her eyes wide with fear and wonder and joy.

The nurse came back in, muttering and mumbling, and took the child out of his mother's arms. "The child hungers!" she scolded. Then she noticed the look on the girl's face. "What ails thee, Mistress? Why — "

But whatever had been there was gone. The young mother turned to the nurse, smiling. "Methinks an angel visited."

The nurse snorted and went out again, the child screeching in her arms.

The girl looked again at the place where the presence had been but saw only reflections of sunlight and shifting shadows. She smiled again, wondering, crossed herself, then went out through a low door into the cobbled street.

1

Meanwhile, at Another Place in Time . . .

UNIPER bent over the low table, carefully lifted the small cardboard pyramid, and examined the objects underneath. The dead mouse was remarkably well preserved, almost mummified, the small portion of rump steak was only slightly green, and the banana was still bright yellow. Satisfied, she put the pyramid down again, setting it exactly within the lines she had drawn on the paper underneath.

She picked up a small cardboard box near the pyramid, held it out at arm's length, and cautiously lifted the lid. The smell was overpowering. She looked in, quickly, glimpsed two wizened objects and a black banana, and clapped the lid back on.

There was a light knock on her bedroom door, and her mother, Marsha, came in. She sniffed and pulled a face. "Am I allowed to ask what you've got in there?" Marsha asked suspiciously. "It smells like a corpse."

"It is," said Juniper cheerfully. "The corpse in the cardboard box is badly decomposed. That's what you can smell. But the mouse in the cardboard pyramid is drying out beautifully, just like a little mummy. It's amazing."

"Fascinating," murmured Marsha, lifting the pyramid. "I see. You've got my dinner in there as well. And I suppose you've got another steak in the box, doing its best to contribute to the noxious stench and rising beautifully to the occasion." She put the pyramid down, carelessly, and Juniper moved it within the lines again.

"It must face magnetic north-south and east-west," she explained, seriously. "Just the same as the Great Pyramid in Egypt. And this is made to the same proportions, too. Those Egyptians knew a few things, Marsha. But it wasn't their embalming that was so clever: it was the shape of the pyramids that preserved the bodies. There's something very special about the space inside a pyramid. I read that someone recently built a pyramid in his back garden, to meditate in, and the neighbours' cats and dogs, which normally lived in a state of war, used to sleep in there together in perfect harmony."

"I hope you're not thinking of building one," Marsha said uneasily. "You're not, are you?"

Juniper gave her a wide, disarming smile. "Of course not. If I build one, it'll be big enough to live in, permanently. I have a theory. I think the pyramid doesn't just slow down decay; I think it actually slows down time. Maybe if we lived in one, we wouldn't get old so fast. Everything would last for years — potted plants, fruit, cut flowers, goldfish. It's worth thinking about. There are things about time that I don't understand. I'm beginning to believe that time as we measure it doesn't even exist. Einstein had a theory about it." She bent over the pyramid again, checking the contents, deep in thought.

Beaten by mental gymnastics, Marsha sighed and sat on the edge of Juniper's four-poster bed. She looked around at all the precious things her daughter loved: the pictures of castles, manor-houses, and tumbling thatched cottages; the brass rubbings from the tombs of knights and noblemen; the tapestries of medieval tournaments and feasts; the large poster of a fourteenth-century knight and his lady; the bunches of dried herbs and flowers; and the beautiful stained glass window of Joan of Arc standing tall and resolute before a medieval town, with banners and white doves flying.

Marsha's eyes moved on to Juniper's face. Juniper was gazing straight ahead, daydreaming, her generous mouth downturned, her dark eyes deep and seeing distant things. Against the stained glass her wild auburn hair danced with fiery lights, and her perfect skin glowed richly in the coloured light.

She is like all the things she admires, thought Marsha: she is sparkling and beautiful, free and strong and self-reliant. And devastatingly difficult at times.

"Has it ever occurred to you, Juniper," she murmured unhopefully, "to be just a normal fourteen-year-old, with pop stars on the walls instead of medieval knights, and plants instead of mummified mice? Can't you just listen to the radio and talk on the phone all day instead of indulging in weird and wonderful practices?"

"No, I can't," said Juniper brightly, putting the pyramid down. "I'm giving up the pyramid experiment, anyway. I've proved what I set out to prove. But I'll never throw out my medieval knights and all my ancient things. I love them. And talking of wonderful practices . . . when are you going to do that telepathic image exchange with me?"

"I haven't time, Juniper. When I'm not looking after this place or working at the florist, I've got my aerobics classes. That image exchange thing would require hours at a time, and even then it'd take months to develop properly. Anyway, I thought you were looking for an artist to do it with. Have you asked Kingsley?"

"No. I won't, now. If I even mention ESP, or anything telepathic, he goes off the deep end. He thinks it's weird. If he phones, I'm not even allowed to say 'Hello, Kingsley,' until he speaks first: it freaks him out. It's very restrictive."

Marsha smiled faintly and stood up. "I'm sure it must be," she said. "You'll find someone else, Juniper. But in the meantime, we still have to eat. And since your pyramid isn't quite as efficient as our refrigerator, I'll go to the shops and get us something fresh for dinner." At the

8

door she turned, remembering something else. "Juniper? Have you done any homework at all this week?"

"Not a lot," admitted Juniper, with a carefree laugh. "I'll have to make do with B's instead of A's for a change."

"That'll shock the system," said Marsha. "How are you getting on with your science teacher now?"

"All right," replied Juniper. "He doesn't call me Doll anymore. And tomorrow we're dissecting rats."

"Right up your alley." Marsha smiled.

"It would be, only I've got to work with Dylan Pidgely, the new boy."

"What's wrong with him?"

Juniper shrugged. "He's a bit of a nerd, that's all. At least he'll behave himself. The last time we did dissections, I worked with Joe Fripps. He spent the whole time trying to look down the front of my shirt."

"You really do have the most appalling problems," muttered Marsha, leaving the room.

When she was gone, Juniper opened her schoolbag and tipped out all her homework. She picked up a maths textbook and sighed. Then she looked up at the calm, determined face of Saint Joan in the coloured glass.

"Well, sister," she said, "if you can climb into all that armour and go off to battle and show an army how to fight, I guess the least I can do is show old Bates how brilliantly I can do battle with his algebra."

2

The Artist Found

HE pale skin peeled back revealing the tidy gut inside — the subtle grey-green of the coiled intestines, the dark scarlet of the liver, and the softer crimson of the tiny heart.

Juniper bent over it, fascinated. "Terrific colours," she said.

There was a faint groan beside her, and she glanced sideways at the boy helping her. He was leaning on the lab bench, his grey eyes half closed behind the steel-rimmed glasses, his lips white. Even his freckles looked pale.

"Don't you pass out, Dylan Pidgely," she muttered. "Don't you dare."

He closed his eyes, swallowed noisily, and shook his head.

"Pick up your pencil, then," she said, returning

her attention to the crucified rat. "You're supposed to be labelling the diagram. Now, watch. This is the small intestine, and that's the stomach. This is the liver. These little yellow things must be globs of fat. And these are the testes. Dylan? Dylan!"

It was too late. He was buckling at the knees, already slithering ungracefully to the floor. Juniper sighed and put down her scalpel. She leaned over Dylan, undid the top button of his shirt, and loosened his collar. She propped him up with his legs bent and his head on his knees. "Get some blood back into your brain cell," she advised, kindly.

One of the boys leaned over from the bench in front, leering, and gave her a grin. "If I faint, will your tender fingers unbutton my shirt?" he asked. She ignored him.

Their teacher arrived and knelt beside Dylan. "Do you think you could walk to the sickroom if someone goes with you?" he asked gently. "The smell of chloroform in here probably isn't helping. Even the walk in fresh air will do you good."

Dylan nodded weakly and staggered to his feet.

"You take him, please, Juniper," said the teacher, "and stay with him for a while."

Juniper collected up Dylan's papers and books and stuffed them roughly into his schoolbag. Then she took his limp arm and led him ceremoniously to the lab door. He lurched unsteadily, and she supported him with her arm. They left to whistles and applause from the rest of the class.

Outside, Juniper glanced sideways into Dylan's white face and smiled. "We hardly know each other," she said, "and here I am, in front of half the relevant world, with you in my arms. This may totally ruin my reputation."

"I'm sorry," he said.

She led him across the asphalt to the office block and into the cool silence of the sickroom. He sat gratefully on the edge of the bed, his head bent.

"I'll be all right, thanks," he said, without looking at her. "You can go now."

She dropped his bag on the polished floor and stood watching him for a while. Her lively black eyes noted his pale skin, the slight ginger of his straight fair hair, and the sensitive curve of his mouth. His eyes were large and pale behind his glasses and were turned slightly down at the outer corners, like a spaniel's. It gave him a permanently sad look. His lashes were unusually long and a deep gold.

"You still look a bit white," she observed. "Why don't you lie down and rest?"

He kicked off his shoes and lay down, dragging the grey blanket over himself.

He wasn't really bad-looking, Juniper decided; just colourless and uninteresting. He'd been in her class a month now, and she'd never seen him angry or excited or laughing. He was quiet and antisocial and lived with his nose in books. He contributed nothing, said nothing. Fainting over a dissected rat was probably the most enthusiastic thing he'd ever done.

"Do you want to read for a while?" she asked.

"I've got a library book in my bag," he replied.

She unzipped his bag and sorted through it. "This one?" she asked, holding it up. She glanced at the title. "*Everyday Life in Medieval England,*" she read. She hesitated and looked sharply at his face. "Are you into medieval things?" she asked.

He nodded slightly and looked out the window. But his face was suddenly tense, and his fingers made tiny nervous folds in the blanket.

Juniper began flicking through the book.

"Give it here," he said suddenly, his voice trembling on the verge of authority.

"In a minute. I'm interested in this sort of thing, too. Some nice illustrations of armour in here." She came to a loose sheet hidden within the pages and took it out. It was a small pencil drawing of a castle, very detailed and accurate, and beautifully done. She felt a rush of excitement, so intense she could hardly breathe.

"This is rather impressive," she said, holding the drawing up and trying to sound calm. "Who did it?"

Dylan stared at her, his eyes wide with alarm.

Her joy plunged. "You stole it," she said.

He shook his head. "No, I didn't. Give it here, please. It's precious."

"I bet it is," she said, holding the drawing close. "It's by a real artist. It's probably quite valuable, even if it is unsigned. Who did it? A friend of yours?"

"I can't say."

"You must be able to say. At least tell me where you found it."

He looked out the window again and said nothing.

"I have to know, Dylan!"

He stared at her, helpless and afraid. "I did it," he said.

"You!"

Juniper sat on the edge of the bed beside him, astounded, the drawing in her hands. It wasn't possible. Not Dylan Pidgely.

"You're not lying, are you?" she asked suspiciously.

"It's one of mine," he said.

She looked at him as if seeing him for the first time. Then she turned to the drawing again, holding it carefully, marvelling at it.

He stole a long look at her bent head. She was leaning over the drawing, her face obscured by her long mass of hair. But he didn't need to see her face. He knew every shade and contour of it, knew the way her eyes changed when she was angry, and the way she tilted back her head when she laughed. He knew what her smile was like; her wide, slow smile that was amused and compassionate and joyful all at once. He knew, though her hair was never tied back, that her ears were twice pierced and she wore tiny purple earrings, and that she had a small mole low on her left cheek and another on her throat.

She looked up from the drawing and gave him a winning smile. "It's Scotney Castle," she said. "You've drawn it perfectly — the island, the lake,

14

the trees, the leadlight windows, and the tower. It's perfect."

"I copied a photo," he said. "I'm not much good at making things up."

For a while she was silent, studying his face. He was uncomfortable under her scrutiny but managed not to look away. She had beautiful eyes, mysterious and deep.

"Are you telepathic, Dylan?" she asked.

"I don't know." He shrugged, considering. "I have vivid dreams, and I know if Bob's unhappy. He's my brother at university."

Juniper gave him the drawing, then stood up and began pacing the room. Dylan threw back the grey blanket, got up, and felt under the bed for his shoes. He began putting them on.

"Will you come to my place?" she asked suddenly. "Sometime over the weekend?"

For a few seconds he didn't move, didn't breathe, even. Then he went on tying his laces, fumbling, his glasses steamed over.

"Will you?" she asked.

He stood up and met her gaze and saw that she was smiling. He swallowed. "What about Kingsley?" he asked.

Her expression didn't alter. "What about him?" she said.

Dylan put the drawing and the book back in his bag, then stood up and pushed his hair out of his eyes. He tried to sound calm. "He's your boyfriend, isn't he?"

"Yes."

"He won't want me around."

"That's an astute observation, Dylan." Her smile widened. "You're discerning as well as being super-sensitive and a brilliant artist."

A slow flush spread upwards from Dylan's neck, and he looked away. He suspected she was laughing at him and couldn't understand why. He was incapable of understanding anything much at the moment.

"Well, will you?" she asked again.

Still he didn't meet her eyes. "All right," he said, "but I've got to mow the lawns and help Dad dig a vegetable garden."

"I only want you for an hour or two," she smiled, "not the whole weekend. Hold out your hand."

He did, cautiously, and she took a pen and wrote something on his wrist.

"My address," she said. "And don't forget, Leonardo da Vinci Pidgely. I've got something very important to propose to you."

And before he could say a word, she was gone.

3

Uncertainties

YLAN stabbed the spade into the soft earth, leaned on it heavily, and wiped his arm across his streaming face. He glanced at his watch. "It's four o'clock, Dad."

Tom Pidgely stopped digging and frowned across the stretch of churned soil. "So? We've got four hours of daylight yet. Don't stop now."

"It's Sunday, too, Dad."

Tom sighed and in a bewildered way passed his hand over his bald patch and through the remaining rim of curly hair. He was a short, stout man with a pleasant face and muscles well developed from weight-lifting in the garage. "So it is," he said. "And I've missed church again. The vicar will be disappointed."

"The weekend's almost over," said Dylan desperately. "I told Juniper I'd go and see her."

His father returned to his digging. "A girl, eh?"

Dylan nodded. "Can I go now?"

"May as well. Can't stand in the path of true love, can I?"

"It's not love, Dad. She's already got a boyfriend. Kingsley Blayd. He's in the Seventh Form. He's the best gymnast in the school. He does modelling, too, for magazines."

Tom stopped digging and faced his son again, frowning, his eyes screwed up against the light. "So what's she want you for, Dylan? Your brains? Goes in for trivial pursuits, does she?"

"She invited me."

"She gave you her address?"

"Yes."

"Are you sure it's for real?"

"I checked in the phone book. M and J Golding, 19 Carradice Drive."

His father gave a low whistle. "You'd better get on your bike, then, hadn't you? And for God's sake, have a shower first."

The shower did nothing at all for Dylan. He came out of it hot, shaking, and dreadfully conscious of time slipping by. In his room he dropped the wet towel on the threadbare carpet, grabbed a clean pair of underpants out of a drawer, and dragged them on. They stuck to his damp skin, and he stretched the elastic yanking them up. He picked his best shirt out of the pile of clothes tossed across the foot of his bed, gave it a good shake, and pulled it on. He pulled on his jeans, dusting off the soil from his latest spin on his bike. He finished dressing, combed his wet hair, and put on his glasses. Immediately they steamed up. He rushed blindly into the lounge.

"I'm going to Juniper's now, Mum."

"Have a nice time, dear." Kathy Pidgely was sitting in a battered orange armchair, knitting and watching television. She was overweight, and her grey hair was sadly in need of another perm. There was an opened packet of biscuits beside her, and she unconsciously reached for it.

"You said you were on another diet, Mum," said Dylan, whipping the packet away and twisting it closed. He threw it onto the sofa across the room.

Kathy sighed. "Well, I've been under a bit of stress lately," she murmured.

"I don't know when I'll be home," said Dylan. "Don't save any dinner for me. I'll get myself some baked beans or something."

His mother studied his face. She had a soft spot for her younger son, even though he wasn't bright like his brother. He was quiet, and he never gave his parents any trouble. For that she was grateful.

"Come here, Dylan," she said.

He sighed but went over to her, and she dabbed at his upper lip with her hanky. "You're sweating, dear," she said. "Stop panicking. She's only a girl."

"She's beautiful, Mum. Half the boys in the school are after a date with her."

"Well, don't get your hopes up. There's got to

19

be a catch in this somewhere. You should have stuck with Helen. She was a nice, dependable girl. She couldn't help having buck teeth."

"How could I stick with her? We moved here. Anyway, she was my cousin."

Kathy sighed heavily and picked up her knitting. "I know. You're not the only one who didn't want to move. Barbara and Robyn had to leave all their friends behind, too. But unemployment's not so bad here. Your father's got a much better chance of getting another job."

Dylan nodded apathetically. He bent and kissed her cheek and hurried out.

On Carradice Drive, Dylan stopped outside number nineteen. He got off his bike, stood it in the driveway, and looked up at the house, his heart thumping. The house was built on a steep slope and had many different levels. It was a pole house, all natural timber, with odd-shaped windows at strange angles, balconies and windowboxes in unexpected places, and stained glass and ivy everywhere.

Dylan checked the number on the letterbox, then looked for the front door. He spotted it at last, tucked into a hidden alcove halfway up the house and reached by a series of wooden stairs. He climbed them, feeling increasingly panic-stricken. Sweat broke out on his palms, and he wished he'd never come.

He knocked on the door. It opened, and a woman stood there, wiping her hands on a small towel. She looked slightly older than Juniper and had the same open face, clear satiny skin, and wide smile. Her hair was a brilliant, chaotic red.

"Hello," she said. "You must be Dylan."

He nodded, speechless. She was wearing tight jeans and a muslin shirt and had a figure like the women in his father's magazines.

Her smile widened, and he noticed that her eyes were blue. "Come in," she said. "I'm Marsha. Juniper's gone for a walk, but she'll be back soon."

He followed her up a tiny passage painted apricot and glowing with amber and green light from three circular windows, and out into a wide kitchen. Everything here was natural wood, even the floors, benches, cupboards, and open shelves.

Marsha went over to the sink and carried on washing vegetables. "What are you like at making coleslaw?" she asked, smiling at Dylan over her shoulder.

"I've never made it," he said.

"Here's the cabbage, and there's the knife. Cut it as finely as you can."

He stood beside her and started hacking into the cabbage. Gently, she took the knife out of his hand. "It's easier if you cut a bit off first and then slice that up into strips," she said, showing him. "That's better. I hope you're staying for dinner, since you're helping to get it."

"Thanks. Only if it suits. Are you Juniper's sister?"

"Thanks for the compliment. I'm her mother."

"Oh. Sorry."

"Don't apologise. Cut that cabbage a bit finer, will you?"

"Sorry. I'm not used to cutting things up."

"So I heard. Not cabbages or rats. You poor thing. I did that once, too, in school. Only I went a bit further and threw up all over the teacher's eyeballs."

Dylan looked horrified, and she laughed. "Not *his* eyeballs, the sheep's. He was dissecting them. I've got no stomach for that sort of thing, either. Juniper has. Reckons she's going to be a surgeon. What do you plan to do?"

"Be a butcher, I guess," he said. "Like Dad."

Marsha shrieked with laughter. Before he could figure out why, Dylan heard the roar of a motorbike outside and then voices. Juniper came in, carrying a bottle of wine and a packet of exotic-looking cheese. She shot Dylan a brilliant smile.

"Hi, Leonardo. I thought you'd chickened out."

He smiled back, flushed and speechless, and put down the knife and the mutilated cabbage.

Behind Juniper was a fair young man in his early twenties, wearing jeans and a leather jacket but no shirt. He was slim and well built, and very good-looking. He went up to Marsha as she stood at the sink, slipped his arms around her waist, and kissed the back of her neck. "Hello, gorgeous," he said. "How are you?"

"Fine. This is a nice surprise."

"I'm inviting myself for dinner. Hope you don't mind. I've brought some wine and your favourite cheese."

"I'm doubly spoilt," said Marsha. "This is Dylan Pidgely. He's staying for dinner, too. Dylan, this is Niall."

Niall put out his hand, and his handshake was firm and warm. "Hello, Dylan. Good to meet you."

"Hello." Dylan managed half a smile. "I didn't realise Juniper had a brother."

Niall gave him a broad grin. "I'm not her brother. I'm Marsha's boyfriend."

Dylan's face flamed, and he turned away. Marsha laughed and put a bottle of gingerbeer and two glasses into Dylan's hands. "Don't be embarrassed," she said softly. "We're not. You and Juniper go and look at books or talk or something, while Niall and I get dinner. I hope you like gingerbeer. Do you?"

He nodded dumbly and followed Juniper into another room.

She took the gingerbeer and glasses from him and placed them on a low table among scattered magazines, shells, pottery, and dishes of large brilliantly painted eggs.

"I really put my foot in it, didn't I?" he said. "Maybe I should just go home."

"Don't be daft. Marsha doesn't care, neither does Niall. Lots of people have younger partners. It's usually the woman who's younger, that's all. Here, have a gingerbeer." She handed him a full glass, and he took it gratefully.

"I thought she was your sister, as well," he mumbled.

"So does everyone. Niall thought we were sisters the first time he saw us. It was at a gypsy fair last summer. He lives in a gypsy caravan, down by the Linsloe River. It's fabulous there. Marsha goes and stays with him sometimes. There's no room for me there. In more ways than one." She grinned and sat on the huge sofa against the wall. It was covered with a large piece of rich green velvet, thrown casually across.

Dylan sat down next to her, sank further than he expected, and tipped half his drink down his shirt. Juniper stood up and went to get him a cloth. She came back and helped him mop up the mess.

"Thanks. Perhaps I'd better keep it handy," he said, putting the cloth on the velvet arm of the sofa, where it spread a dark stain.

Juniper looked at him sideways, half smiling, and sighed. "Dylan Pidgely, you're priceless," she said.

"Is that why you asked me here?"

"It's one reason."

"What's the other?"

Juniper looked down at her hands and was silent, her straight dark eyebrows drawn together in a slight frown. She was wearing grey jeans and a black T-shirt, with a fine silver chain about her neck. Against the black her skin glowed, and a faint pulse throbbed in her throat. Her hair hid her face again, but Dylan was keenly aware of her unease. He had an intense longing to help her but didn't know how.

She got up and walked across the polished floor

to the bay window, and for a while stood with her back to him, looking out. He waited, tense and amazed that somehow he was the cause of her discomfort.

She turned and sat on the edge of the window-seat, between the rich velvet and silk cushions. Against the luminous textures and colours she looked dark and cool, her face shadowed, the edges of her hair red-gold against the light. She looked small and vulnerable and almost afraid. She was still holding her empty glass, and her fingers were white and tense. She lifted her chin, took a deep breath, and looked straight into Dylan's face.

"There's something I want to do with you," she said. "Something I've never done before."

Dylan's glasses started to steam over. He took them off, slowly, and polished them carefully on his shirt. Then he put them on again and stared straight ahead, past her shoulder and into the dazzling evening light.

"You'd better tell me," he said huskily.

4

The Proposal

HAT I want to do," said Juniper, "is an experiment in mental telepathy." She hesitated, waiting for his reaction. There wasn't one. "I know I have some telepathic abilities," she went on more confidently. "I can go through a pack of cards, face down, and guess about fifteen correctly. And I often know who it is when the phone rings before I answer it. But I want to try mental telepathy with someone else. I want to try giving someone else my thoughts. Images are easier to receive than words. They're more intuitive somehow, not so tied up in logic and reason. I want to see if I can send images to someone else and whether they can draw what they receive. I need someone who's sensitive and a good artist."

His gaze shifted, and his eyes met hers. "Me, you mean?" he said.

She smiled unexpectedly. "Who else, Leonardo? You're perfect."

"What's wrong with Kingsley? He won that school competition for art."

"That's only because you didn't enter. You don't even take art for a subject, goodness knows why."

"Because I didn't think I was any good. It's the only thing I enjoy: that and reading. I don't want my stuff criticised. It's bad enough being useless at English and science and sports and woodwork and cooking and everything else, without having my art torn to shreds as well."

"Nobody's criticising your art," she said. "You don't have to get defensive with me. I think your art's terrific. And I won't tell a soul about it, if that's what you want. Will you try this with me?"

He shrugged. "Why don't you do it with Kingsley?"

"He doesn't believe in ESP."

"What about your other friends, then? You've got plenty."

"I don't want one of them. I want you."

He looked away again, his palms hot and damp. "I don't know," he said.

She crossed the room and sat beside him, close. "Please, Dylan. I really want to try this. It means a lot to me. If you're worried about Kingsley, don't be. He might be my boyfriend, but he doesn't own me. If I want to try telepathic communication with you, I will. If Kingsley doesn't like it, that's his problem."

Neither of them said anything for a while. Then he asked: "This telepathic thing. Is it dangerous?"

"No. It's communicating without words, that's all. Animals do it all the time. So do people really close to each other, like twins, and close friends. It's nothing evil or dark, Dylan. I want to use my total brain, that's all; to explore the God-given intuitions we were born with. It's an imaginative thing, like meditating, or painting, or visualising a scene in a book. It's a positive, joyful thing. A game."

He sighed, torn between fear of the unknown and the desire to spend more time with her. He looked sideways into her face and saw that her lips were slightly parted, her magnificent eyes bright and intense. Her dark hair was like a soft cloud about her face, and tiny tendrils curled on the edges of her forehead. Dylan's glasses started to steam over again, and he took them off.

"All right," he said. "I'll do it."

Juniper's smile was triumphant and lovely. She leaned over and gave him a soft kiss on the cheek.

"Thanks, Leonardo," she said. "You're a special human being."

He blushed. "I wish I were," he said.

With a dramatic flourish, Niall threw his king of diamonds onto the table. "Beat that, Dylan, if you can!" he said.

Dylan glanced at Juniper, on his left. She met his gaze calmly, her face inscrutable. He wondered if she knew what cards he had.

"Don't worry," she said. "I can't read them."

"That disappoints me," said Niall. "You win cards so often, I thought you must be clairvoyant. That's why I wanted you for a partner this time."

Dylan played his jack of diamonds, and Marsha laughed. "We've won again, Dylan!" she said. "For someone who's never played five hundred before, you've done brilliantly."

Juniper threw her last useless card on the table and gave Dylan a glance tinged with grudging admiration. "It's time you went home, Leonardo," she said.

Dylan looked at his watch and was surprised. It was almost one A.M.

"I'll make us a drink first," said Marsha, standing up. "Coffee for you, Dylan? Or there's cocoa, herbal tea, or Chinese tea."

"Chinese tea, please," said Dylan, feeling adventurous.

"Tell me, why does Juniper call you Leonardo?" asked Niall.

"Because I draw," said Dylan.

"Leonardo da Vinci stuff," explained Juniper, waving her hand towards a large print on the wall. "You should have seen the castle he did, Niall. It was fantastic."

Dylan got up and went over to the print and looked at it closely.

"It's called *The Virgin of the Rocks*," said Juniper. "I like it better than *Mona Lisa*. She looks a bit of a wimp, to me."

Dylan's eyes were on the painting. "It's beautiful," he said. "It's deep. There's a whole world behind those rocks. I love his colours. He's made his babies look a bit too intelligent, though."

"They're allowed to be," said Juniper. "They're John the Baptist and Jesus Christ."

Dylan grinned. "I'll forgive him, then."

"I've got a book of Leonardo's paintings if you want to borrow it," Juniper said. "Did you know he was a musician as well? And a scientist and an engineer. He designed an aeroplane four centuries before the first one was built."

Dylan sat down beside her and gave her a wide smile. It was the first time she had ever seen him smile, and she was pleasantly surprised. His whole face had been transformed.

"And you've named me after him," Dylan murmured, awed. "After a genius. I can cope with that."

"You're going to have to cope with a lot more than that," she said. "We haven't even started yet, Dylan Pidgely."

Niall laughed. "Sounds serious, Leo," he said. "You'd better organise your defences and get out your war paint. You're going to need it. And if it's ever prudent to retreat for a while, you can come and stay with me. My caravan needs repainting."

Dylan didn't know whether to laugh or not. He

30

decided not to. "Thanks," he said. "I'd like to be a gypsy for a while." He looked at Niall curiously. "What do you do all day, Niall? You don't work, do you? Don't you get bored?"

"Oh, I do work," replied Niall, amused. "I sit under the willow trees and I do bone carvings and make jewellery. I sell enough to buy food. I sew most of my own clothes, bake my own bread. It's a frantic existence, but it has its good points. I don't have appliances that break down, or bills to pay, or a boss to tell me what to do. I catch fish in the mornings, sleep in the sun, play my flute, write a bit of poetry, and love Marsha in the afternoons. I can't think of a better way to celebrate life."

Dylan smiled. He couldn't imagine his father loving his mother in the afternoons. Or anytime.

"What do your people do?" asked Niall.

Dylan shrugged. "Nothing, really. They watch TV a lot. Dad's unemployed. Mum does house-work for an old lady up the road. She sends most of her money to Bob at university. He's going to be a lawyer. I've got twin sisters, Barbara and Robyn. They're six. I look after them while Mum's working."

Marsha came in with the drinks and handed Dylan his tea. "I heard you say your father's un-employed," she said. "I'd pay him to do a bit of maintenance work around here, if he's interested. Is he any good at painting? My windowsills need sanding down and painting again."

"He can do anything," said Dylan.

"He's Leonardo's father, remember," said Niall. "He'd probably build you a helicopter if you wanted one. I'll do your painting, love. You don't have to employ someone."

Marsha gave him his coffee and a tender smile. "I've seen your painting," she said. "You're not getting anywhere near my windowsills. Not unless you're climbing over them at two in the morning. Do you think your father would be interested, Dylan?"

"Bound to be," said Dylan, "especially if there's money involved."

"Tell him to phone me sometime, then," said Marsha.

"That's marvellous, that is," grumbled Juniper. "How can Dylan and I do anything with his father creeping around and peering in all the windows?"

"He won't be peering, he'll be painting," said Marsha. "And if you and Dylan want privacy, you can go up to the attic. His father'd have trouble creeping around that window."

Dylan choked on his tea and spilt it all down his trousers. Juniper rushed for the cloth again, and he mopped himself up.

"I think I'd better get going," he mumbled, his face scarlet. "Thanks for the dinner, Mrs Golding. It was great."

"You're very welcome," she replied. "And please call me Marsha. I hope we see you again soon. It's nice having someone else winning at cards for a change, instead of Juniper."

Juniper walked down the steps to the road with

Dylan and waited while he got on his bike. "When will I see you again?" she asked.

"At school tomorrow, I guess."

"I mean, here."

He thought frantically. "Tuesday. No, the twins have swimming then. It'll have to be Wednesday. No — Thursday. Definitely Thursday."

"Thursday? ' 'Tis twenty years till then!' " she cried. She could see his blush, even in the dark. "Shakespeare," she explained, laughing. "Juliet to Romeo, when they parted."

There was nothing he could say to that, so he shot her a brief smile and pedalled away.

5

The Gift

HEN Dylan arrived at Juniper's that Thursday, the door was open wide and he could hear music from somewhere deep inside the house. He knocked several times, uncomfortably aware of the afternoon sun burning through his shirt and of his palms wet with sweat. He wiped his hot face on his sleeve and knocked again.

Juniper appeared, glowing golden and green as she came towards him past the stained glass windows. She was wearing a thin white cotton dress and looked luminous and cool.

"Hello, Leonardo," she said. "You're late. I thought you weren't coming."

"Dad wasn't home, after all," he explained, following her through the mottled light and out into the kitchen. "I had to arrange with a neighbour to look after the twins, and then I fell off my bike. I've bent the front wheel. I had to carry it back home, then walk here."

"You didn't hurt yourself?" she asked, handing him a glass of chilled apple juice.

"Thanks. No."

"You're not nervous, are you?" she asked gently. "You look . . . ruffled."

He finished the juice and put the glass down carefully, so she wouldn't notice how his hand shook. "No," he said. "I'm not nervous. I've just been rushing around, that's all."

"We could have left this for another day," she said.

He met her eyes and grinned. "Not in a million years. This is the only good thing in my week."

"I hope it is good and not a total disaster," she said. "Nothing is certain in telepathic things, you know. You'd better come upstairs. I've got the paper and pencils for you up in the attic. I bought the best I could find."

He followed her up several short flights of stairs, past glimmering alcoves and landings with stained glass windows and soft wall-hangings, past several closed doors on different levels and a bathroom with a tiled bath sunk low into the floor. The whole house glowed with the warmth of natural wood and smelled fragrant. There were flowers everywhere, even in pottery bowls on the corners of stairways.

"I love your home," he said, as they climbed the last flight of stairs. "It's like being inside a huge tree."

35

"You'll love this room," she said, opening the attic door. "It's special."

He went in and knew what she meant. It was a small room, but the large low window and the sweeping windowseat gave it an illusion of space. The seat was covered with cushions of purple velvet, vivid in all the gold. The whole room was a semicircle, wide and curving and flooded with light. An oval rug made a violet and blue pool on the floor, and there was a bowl of white blossoms on the windowsill. The ceiling was low and sloped down towards the window. The room was bare save for a few sheets of paper in the centre of the floor, several pencils and an eraser, and the bowl of flowers.

"Marsha comes here to meditate," explained Juniper. "She calls it her High Place, and no one is allowed in here without her permission. She only lets people in here who have good vibrations."

"I'm honoured, then," he said, smiling, stooping slightly to look out the low window. He saw only treetops, a few roofs, and the sea in the distance, shining.

When he faced Juniper again he was changed somehow, more assured and at peace with himself. "This is a beautiful place," he murmured. "I used to dream about a room like this."

He crouched on the floor by the paper, felt its texture and weight, and nodded, surprised and pleased. "It's French," he said. "Made from fabric. You must have paid the earth for it."

"You're worth it, Leonardo," she said, perching

on the edge of the windowseat. "Now sit down, and I'll tell you what we're going to do."

Dylan sat on the rug, the paper blank and luminous in front of him, a pencil in his hands. He glanced at his watch. It was one minute to six. Juniper had been gone for half an hour. He had no idea where she'd gone. She could be on the other side of town if she'd taken her bike. In another minute she'd be sending him an image. He toyed with the pencil, absent-mindedly, then remembered he was supposed to be preparing himself. He closed his eyes and tried to concentrate.

He could hear crickets outside and a lawnmower somewhere. A heavy truck roared up a distant hill, and the sun poured across his hands, warming them. He tried to breathe slowly, the way she'd told him to, but he got panic feelings and was terrified of failing, of seeing nothing, doing nothing. He wished she'd bought some cheap drawing paper after all, in case he made awful mistakes. He didn't dare look at his watch again. It must be after six by now. Long after.

Peace, my soul, he thought. Relax. Think of nothing. Be empty, receptive, like the paper there.

He half opened his eyes and looked at the paper through his long gold lashes. The whiteness flickered and glowed, moved with half-formed shadows, and was empty again. The lawnmower stopped, and he relaxed. The peace became vibrant, joyous. Without his trying, his breath slowed until it was almost imperceptible. Yet he was not sleepy; his mind was alert and waiting. The paper moved again, floating with images like dreams.

His heartbeat quickened, and his fingers tightened around the pencil. His eyelids flickered open, and his hand moved towards the paper, calmly and with purpose.

Not too many details this first time, she had said; just shapes and lines. Keep it simple, be aware of the whole form, the full view.

Circles seemed to swirl in his mind, not unpleasantly. There was a sensation of perfect, peaceful wholeness, unbroken and smooth. He drew them, as accurately as if they had been done with a compass: three circles, side by side.

Something blurred in his mind, became out of focus and, in a way, almost out of tune. It was as if he were listening to a radio, and it wasn't quite tuned in properly. The waves were distorted. There was something wrong with the circles. No. Not with the circles themselves, but with the placement of them. He drew them again, overlapping them, setting them slightly one above the other. The blurring in his mind became clear, focused, and totally in tune. He smiled to himself, pleased. I've got the circles, Juniper, he thought. Now I'm ready for the rest of it.

There was a long line, perfectly straight, going completely through the circle on the right. Then another line, almost parallel. Then he felt the blurring again and the jangled vibrations. He erased the second line and drew it again, joining it to the base of the first line, slightly below the circles, and leaning it out at a slight angle. He drew other lines, fanning them out over the circles with equal angles in between.

That's a weird building, he thought, if that's what it is. Maybe it's a mural of some kind, or graffiti. No guessing, she'd said, no speculation, no judgements; they put up barriers. Just receive and record.

So he recorded what came to him, sometimes correcting, sometimes drawing with a certainty and accuracy that amazed him. He knew that what he drew was not what he planned or imagined. It came to him from outside, surprising and delighting him.

When it was over he dropped the pencil and covered his face with his hands. He was shaking, totally exhausted, almost too tired to look at the finished form. When he did look, he was disappointed.

It was nothing he recognised. It was an abstract design, a pattern of circles and lines and crescents, balanced on a single point. It was pleasing to look at, but meaningless.

He stood up shakily and pushed open one of the windows. The shadows in the garden were long, and the sun was low and dazzling behind the trees. He looked at his watch. Seven-thirty! He was supposed to get dinner again tonight.

He turned and saw Juniper standing there, the drawing in her hands. He hadn't heard her arrive.

Slowly, she bent and placed the drawing carefully on the floor. He waited, his hands tense at

39

his sides, his eyes searching her face. "Well?" he said.

She suddenly spun in a wild, joyous dance, hugging herself. "We did it, Leonardo!" she laughed, exultant. "We did it!"

He sat on the edge of the windowseat, feeling suddenly weak. She sat beside him and smiled into his astounded face. "We did it, you and I," she said. "Better than I ever had hoped."

"I'm glad," he said, smiling faintly. "But what exactly did we do?"

"The sculpture in St Stephen's Park. Just around the corner."

"There isn't a sculpture there."

"There is now. They must have put it up yesterday."

"I've never seen it."

"Neither had I, until today. You drew it perfectly, Dylan. Well, almost perfectly. It had seven rays going out, not ten. And the middle circle was slightly higher than the other two. And those crescents were really birds flying, and there were only three of them. The sculpture symbolises freedom. It's beautiful. And you're terrific."

For a while they looked at each other without speaking. Between them spun something awesome, something astounding and enigmatic, that bound them together more than any word or touch. For a few moments they were overwhelmed by it and almost afraid; then Juniper smiled again, and the power subsided.

Dylan took off his glasses and rubbed his eyes

with his fingertips. When he looked up again he was frowning, his grey eyes troubled.

"Do you really know what we're doing?" he asked.

"Of course I do," she replied. "We're using our total brain, exercising to the full our natural gift of inner sight. All we're doing is living to our fullest potential. Don't you see, Dylan? This could change our lives."

He gave her a slow, uncertain smile. "That's what I'm afraid of."

"I don't often see you with your glasses off," she said softly. "You've got beautiful eyes, Dylan. And a nice smile, when you manage one."

His smile spread, lighting his whole face. Then he blushed deeply and put his glasses back on. Suddenly he leapt to his feet.

"The potatoes!" he cried. "I'm supposed to cook the potatoes!"

He rushed out, and she heard him clattering down the stairs. She yelled after him: "When?"

He stopped and gazed up through the kaleidoscope of light. "When what?" he asked.

"When are you coming back?"

"In twenty years," he called. "The weekend. Tonight. Give me an hour."

At ten that night he phoned her.

"Hello, Dylan," she said, before he said a word.

He was taken aback for a moment, then he laughed. "I forgot," he said. "I didn't mean what

41

I said about an hour or the weekend. Will tomorrow night be all right?"

"Tomorrow will be terrific," she replied.

He hesitated. "You're not going out somewhere with Kingsley?"

"I was." Her voice was warm. "But I'll cancel that. Will you stay for dinner, too?"

"If that's all right with your Mum."

"I'm sure it'll be very all right."

"Good night, then."

"Leonardo? Would you like me to send you some dreams?"

He was silent for a long time. "Ah . . . maybe not," he said huskily. "I have enough trouble with my own dreams without having yours as well." He was having trouble with his pulse rate, too.

There was a delighted chuckle from her end. "You're a chicken, Leonardo. Good night."

6

Expectations

YLAN sighed, tore off the used portion of the drawing paper, and screwed it up. He closed his eyes, took several deep breaths, and opened his eyes again. A sparrow was fluttering on the window ledge outside, trying to capture an insect on the glass. Dylan watched for a while, then dragged his attention back to the paper in front of him.

Nothing.

Panic overwhelmed him. Suddenly he was afraid. He was afraid that he'd fail and afraid that he wouldn't; afraid that he wasn't really telepathic and afraid that he was. Part of him hoped that yesterday's triumph was a coincidence, a freak chance; and another part of him longed desperately to repeat it again and again, to please Juniper.

He wrestled the fears aside and tried earnestly to clear his mind. Relax, he thought, desperately. Count to twenty. Do some deep breathing.

After a while he thought he saw star shapes and drew them carefully on the paper. Beautiful stars they were, with five perfect points, the background softly shaded to make the edges glow. He saw a form, nebulous and wavering. He drew an outline, an irregular shape like a face in profile. Interesting. He shaded it carefully. Dark hair, strong jaw-line, and a firm, determined mouth. It looked vaguely familiar. "Kingsley Blayd!" he said aloud. He tore the profile off, ripped it into several pieces, and threw them across the room.

He got a clean sheet of paper and started again. He drew for a long time, then sat back, satisfied. He looked again and swore. If she could make anything out of that lot, she'd be more than telepathic. She'd be a magician.

He got up, disgusted, and went downstairs to the lounge. Marsha was there, reading a book.

"Hello, Dylan. You've been quiet. I didn't realize you were here. Where's Juniper?"

He shrugged and sat down on the sofa beside her. Automatically, he looked for the television set. There wasn't one. He picked up one of the painted eggs and examined it.

"I don't know where Juniper is," he said. "I guess she'll be back soon."

Marsha gave him a bewildered look and shook her head. "An exhilarating relationship you two have," she said. "I hope she left you some books to read while she wandered off."

"I've been drawing in the attic."

"I hope you've been happy, then."

"Not really. It didn't turn out." He turned the egg over in his hands, admiring it. It was a large egg made of papier-mâché and painted a deep, vivid blue. Over the blue were painted in finest detail medieval knights jousting and many-towered castles and dragons flying against silver moons. "This is beautiful," he said, momentarily forgetting the disaster in the attic. "Who made it?"

"A friend of Niall's. He made the others as well. They're dragons' eggs. He gave them to Juniper for her birthday."

"You've got lots of beautiful things here," observed Dylan, still looking at the egg and tracing the pictures with his fingers.

After a while Marsha asked: "What sort of things do you draw, Dylan?"

"Medieval things," he replied.

"Is that what you're drawing for Juniper? Something medieval?"

"I wish I were. I don't know what I'm supposed to be drawing at the moment."

"Sounds intriguing."

He glanced at her and half smiled. "We're exchanging images telepathically," he said.

"And it works?"

Dylan's face broke into one of its rare, bright smiles. "It did yesterday. I screwed up today."

"Why?"

"Scared, I suppose."

"I'm not surprised. That's some gift, Dylan. Do you think you can handle it?"

"I guess so. I won't know unless I try."

"Be careful, won't you?" Marsha said, and he looked at her, surprised. She hesitated a moment, then went on, "Keep your feet on the ground, Dylan. Juniper has a habit of flying off in her own marvellous directions and expecting everyone else to trail along after her. But this is a special thing you're doing. Don't let her have her own way all the time. You be the one in control."

"I'll do my best," he said gravely.

"I'm sure you will," she smiled. "May I see what you did yesterday? Or is it private?"

"No, it's not private. I'll go and get it."

He raced upstairs but stopped when he came to the attic. He stared at the mutilated drawings, then went and crouched in front of them, all his disappointment and fear and rage rushing back. They were a mass of garish, broken lines, deformed shapes, and coarse, angry shadows. They were nothing. Worse than nothing. A mockery, a blot on all his dreams. He screwed them up violently and threw them across the room. Twenty dollars worth of French drawing paper, ruined. To say nothing of his soul. And Juniper's smile. She'd probably kill him and never ask him back again. You take control, Marsha had said. He thought bitterly, I can't even control a pencil, let alone a girl like Juniper.

He sighed wearily and looked under the unused papers for yesterday's drawing. It was there, kept flat and safe. In one corner, in tiny, beautiful script, she'd written yesterday's date, the time they had transferred the image, and the words: "First Result. Image sent: sculpture in St Stephen's Park." He removed the drawing and took it downstairs to Marsha.

She had cleared a space on the table ready for it. She stared at it, puzzled. "What is it, Dylan?"

"It's that new sculpture in the park," he explained.

Recognition dawned, and Marsha laughed. "So it is! There was a photo of it in the paper last night. I suppose those half moons are the birds. Heavens, that's amazing! And you drew this without ever having seen the sculpture? Just from what Juniper sent you telepathically?"

He nodded. "Not bad, is it?"

"Not bad? It's incredible!"

The front door banged, and after a minute Juniper came in. She looked flushed and on edge, and angry. She glanced at the drawing on the table, then at Dylan. He noticed that the dark of her eyes had deepened, and he swallowed nervously.

"What's that doing here?" she asked.

"I was showing Marsha what we did yesterday," he said. "I didn't think it would matter."

"Well, it does. We'll have enough trouble living up to our own expectations over all this without worrying about other people's as well."

"I don't have any expectations," said Marsha.

"I won't even ask questions if you don't want me to. And there's no need to talk to Dylan like that. It's his drawing. He can do what he likes with it."

Juniper looked at Dylan, and her eyes softened. "Do you mind if we don't look at today's drawings just yet? I need some time by myself."

"That's all right," he said. He hesitated. "What's wrong, Juniper?"

"Everything," she said, and went upstairs to her room.

Dylan sat down, feeling suddenly empty and depressed, and stared at the drawing without seeing it. Marsha sat beside him.

"You mustn't let Juniper's feelings get to you," she said quietly. "Her images that she wants to send, yes; but not her moods or problems."

"I can't help it," he said.

"You can, and I think it's important that you do. What you and Juniper are doing is something special and wonderful. But it can make you closer, perhaps, than you really want to be. It's a very powerful thing, Dylan. Keep it in perspective. She's upset about something. That's her problem, not yours or mine. She'll be moody tonight and won't talk much. But that's her choice. You and I can get dinner and have a few laughs, and with a bit of luck the weather in this house might improve."

He gave her a crooked grin. "Would you like me to make the coleslaw?" he asked.

Marsha hesitated, then smiled. "I guess I can risk it if the cabbage can," she said.

7

Dylan's Troubles

OM Pidgely watched until the television station closed down for the night, then got up and turned the switch off. He looked at his watch, frowning. He sat down again, his hands clenched on the arms of his chair, his eyes fixed on the bright floral wallpaper ahead. The large orange and yellow flowers irritated him intensely, and he shifted his gaze to the painting above the fireplace. That was worse. He hated those prints of glassy-eyed snivelling kids with tears on their cheeks. Kathy had no taste when it came to interior decorating. Usually that didn't bother him, but tonight it did.

Tonight the whole house bothered him. He detested the old weatherboard box, the garish wallpapers, the gloomy passage down to the red and grey kitchen, the faded rose-spangled carpets, and

49

the shabby furniture. He hated his own power-
lessness in the face of unemployment and his ina-
bility to provide more for his family.

Glowering, he slumped lower in his chair and
waited.

Three hours he waited.

There was a scuffle outside and the clatter of
the garden rake as someone tripped over it. There
was a brief silence, a loud hiccup, and another
scuffle. The handle of the front door turned, cautiously, and someone crept inside.

Tom's hands tightened on the chair and he called
loudly, "Come in here, Dylan."

Silence and total stillness. Then another hiccup.
The lounge door was slowly pushed open, and
Dylan stood there, swaying slightly.

" 'Morning, Dad."

"Come here."

Dylan shuffled in, his head bent, his face slightly
averted. His hair was dishevelled, and he had
damp stains all up his sleeves.

"Shut the door, Dylan."

Dylan closed the lounge door and backed carefully to a chair. He sat down gingerly and gave
his father an apologetic grin. "Did you wait up for
me, Dad?"

"No. I've been sitting here on the chance that
I might catch the odd burglar. Where have you
been?"

"At Juniper's."

"Do you know what time it is?"

"Ah . . . must be nearly midnight."

"It's nearly breakfast."

"Can't be. We just finished dinner."

"Don't get smart, Dylan. You're in enough trouble already. You were supposed to take Barbara to the doctor yesterday. She's been crying with earache. And this is the second time you've sneaked in here in the small hours. What have you been doing?"

"Dishes. I stayed to help do the dishes. Juniper kept breaking things. She got kind of agitatit . . . agintated . . . agid . . . twitchy. So I helped Marsha."

"Come here, Dylan."

Dylan got up unsteadily and went to stand in front of his father. Tom peered at him. Dylan looked unnaturally flushed, and his eyes were slightly crossed.

"Can you stand up straight?" asked Tom.

"It'sh difficult, Dad."

"You've been drinking, haven't you?"

"Marsha'n'me had a bottle of wine."

"Who's Marsha?"

"Jupiter's mother."

"Juniper's?"

"Yeah. Her's."

"I'm not very impressed with you, Dylan. I'll talk to you in the morning about this. And I'll see this Marsha woman."

"She wants to see you, Dad. It's her windows."

"What about them?"

"Can't remember. Something to do with creeping in."

51

"She's had a burglar?"

"No. A gypsy."

"Oh, for God's sake, Dylan, go to bed."

"Good night, Dad." He staggered off, and Tom slumped forward in the chair, his face buried in his hands. After a while he began to chuckle. Then he got up, turned out the light, and went down the pitch-black passage. As he passed Dylan's room he pushed open the door and peered in. Dylan was lying flat on his back in the dimness, fully clothed, snoring. He had a blissful smile on his face.

Juniper knelt in the glimmering half-light of the attic and picked up a fragment of one of the drawings Dylan had torn. It was a portion of a face in profile. She picked up the other scattered pieces and took them over to the pale dawn light on the windowseat. She spread the papers out, smoothing them carefully with her hands, then pieced them neatly together.

It was a face. Kingsley Blayd's. For a few moments she stared, astounded. Then she spread the pieces carefully one on top of the other, in order. Later she'd glue them together again.

Then her eye fell on the other crumpled drawings on the floor, and she spread those out, too, taking care not to smudge the pencilwork. She took them over to the window to look at them. She saw the slashes of dark, angry lines and meaningless, shadowed forms. And the stars. She leaned forward, intent, her eyes wide.

No, she thought. It couldn't be. Dylan couldn't possibly be that good.

She let out a long breath and leaned back against the window, tensely. She was shivering and felt slightly sick. After a while she got up and spread the drawings on the floor, placing the torn portrait on the top. She picked up a pencil and wrote at the bottom of each drawing, in shaky script: "Second Result. These, plus torn portrait of K.B. Image sent: none, consciously. Was interrupted by K.B. and angry. Stars were on K.B.'s sweatshirt."

Dylan slammed the bathroom door shut, winced, and snapped the lock. From the other side came screams and sobs and a small foot kicking the door furiously.

"That's enough, Robyn!" yelled Kathy from the kitchen, banging the frypan on the stove. "Just wait your turn. Come here and help make the toast."

"I want Mrs Tiffany!" howled Robyn, scrabbling at the bathroom lock.

Dylan bent over the bath, groaning, and picked the bedraggled rubber doll from the soapy puddle along the bottom. He opened the door and hurled the doll out. It thudded against the opposite wall and Robyn screamed. "You'll hurt her feelings!"

"Why not?" yelled Dylan, slamming the door again. "You drown her every night!"

Robyn went away, grumbling and crooning to the doll, and Dylan leaned over the handbasin, his eyes closed. He bent his forehead against the cool glass of the wall mirror and sighed.

Then he laughed softly to himself. But it had been a great night, he thought, even if Juniper had been upset. They'd listened to compact discs until ten, and then they'd had dinner. Juniper had been all right by the time they ate, though she'd seemed restless and agitated. Marsha had some terrific music. It was music by people Dylan had never heard of — amazing electronic music, rich and deep and more powerful than anything he'd ever heard. It was music that evoked images and colours and emotions, and had given his soul wings. And the sound had been astounding. It was nothing like the scratched records his parents played. Last night's music had been crystal clear and shining, and utterly beautiful. And Marsha hadn't minded that he'd just sat there and listened, transported and joyful to the point of tears, half drunk with harmony and wine. What a night.

He finished washing, decided he didn't need a shave, and left the bathroom. His father met him just outside and gave him a wink.

"Feeling all right, Bacchus?"

Dylan grinned. "Never better, Dad."

At the breakfast table Kathy banged a plate of greasy fried eggs in front of him and frowned at his bleary eyes. "What time did you get in last night, Dylan?"

"It's okay, dear, I've already talked to him," murmured Tom from behind the newspaper. "He won't be that late again."

"He looks awful," said Kathy.

"He always looks awful," said Robyn cheerfully.

"Just be quiet and eat your breakfast," said Tom, putting down the paper and picking up his knife and fork.

Barbara glared at Dylan across the checked cloth and rubbed her right ear.

Guiltily, Dylan stabbed his fried eggs. "I'll take you to the doctor today, Barbie," he said.

"It'll be weekend rates, today," said Kathy. "I suppose you'll get a job, Dylan, to help pay for the extra."

"I'm sorry," muttered Dylan, putting down his knife and fork. It was going to be one of those mealtimes.

"It's all right, dear," said Tom peaceably. "I've got a job building an aviary down the road. That'll bring in a bit more."

Kathy looked up sharply. "And how long is that job going to last?" she asked. "Building birdcages isn't enough, Tom. You might think it's fun wandering around the neighbourhood doing odd jobs for grateful solo mums, but it doesn't pay the power bill. The last one was over a hundred and twenty dollars. And the rates are due next month. What are we supposed to do?"

"We could have a few candlelight dinners," said Tom, picking up the paper again. "I wouldn't object."

"That's typical," said Kathy. "Avoid the issue. Pretend we haven't got a power bill. Light a few candles, open another tin of spaghetti, we'll eat Italian tonight, and ask old Mr Shirazi next door to come in and play us his violin."

"Sounds nice," said Dylan seriously, and his mother glared at him.

"If you've finished breakfast, go and mow the lawns," she said.

Dylan poured himself a glass of milk, and Robyn pulled his uneaten eggs over to her place. "I like Mr Shirazi," she said, eagerly. "He's got hairs up his nose and long yellow fingernails. Can he bring his dog?"

"That's enough," said Tom, turning to another page in the paper. "Your mother was joking. Hey — here's a job for a night watchman at that new plastics factory."

"Night work?" asked Kathy. "You want to do night work?"

"Why not?" said Tom. "You wouldn't miss me."

Dylan finished his milk and left the table.

"Put something on your feet!" Kathy called after him. "I'm not having you mow your feet off."

Dylan got his sneakers and went outside.

He was halfway through the lawns when Barbara screamed at him from the kitchen window. "Dylan! The phone! It's your girlfriend!"

Dylan stopped the mower and raced inside, scattering lawn clippings all along the passage and leaving green skidmarks on the kitchen linoleum. He grabbed the receiver. "Hello? Juniper?"

" 'Tis me, and none other," she said, and he

could tell she was smiling. "Do you always do heavy breathing down the phone, Leonardo, this early in the morning?"

"I'm mowing the lawns."

"Oh. For a minute there I got quite fluttery. Would you like to come around this afternoon?"

"For some more drawing?"

"Naturally. I think we'll give the wine a miss this time."

"It didn't work yesterday."

"I thought it worked very well. You were quite squiffy when you left."

"I meant the drawing. That didn't work."

"It did, actually, Leonardo. I'll explain when you get here."

He was silent for a moment or two, still panting. Then he said, "Will two o'clock be all right?"

"Two will be wonderful. I'll see you then."

He blushed and hung up and turned to see the twins watching him.

"You do *drawings* for her?" Barbara asked. "Pictures?"

Dylan ignored them and got himself a glass of water.

"What do you draw?" asked Robyn slyly. "Rude things?"

"Yes. Mickey Mouse without his trousers on," Dylan said, and went back to the lawns.

8

"Dylan Pidgely, You're Amazing"

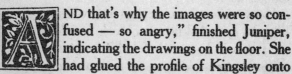ND that's why the images were so confused — so angry," finished Juniper, indicating the drawings on the floor. She had glued the profile of Kingsley onto a sheet of purple card, so perfectly the joins could hardly be seen. "I honestly didn't know he was going to be at the library," she added. "I wanted to send you impressions of shelves of books and that big spiral staircase going up to the second floor. They would have made distinctive lines to draw. Next time I'll go where I'm less likely to meet someone I know."

Dylan gathered up the drawings and filed them in the thick cardboard folder she'd made for them. He propped it against the back wall of the attic. "Why were you so angry, though?" he asked, curiously. "He wasn't to know you were trying to send telepathic messages."

"He was with Dianne Winthrop," she replied shortly. "And now I'm going, Dylan. Give me until four. I'll start sending you an image then, right on the dot."

He looked at his watch. "But that's ages away!"

"I know. I may be late home afterwards, too. Tell Marsha for me. She's at aerobics this afternoon. You'll stay for dinner again, won't you? You won't leave before I get back?"

"I'll be here," he promised.

At the door she hesitated and turned back. "Dylan? Have you noticed when you're receiving images that your pulse rate goes up?"

"Yes," he replied thoughtfully. "It does, actually. My breathing slows down, but my heart starts going mad."

"I read something interesting in a book once," she said. "When two people are making a telepathic exchange, their hearts beat at exactly the same rate. It must be something to do with body energies and vibrations. Take your pulse this time, exactly half an hour after you start drawing. At four-thirty. And I'll take mine." She paused, smiling. "You do know how to take your pulse, don't you?"

"Sure," he said, gripping his left forearm tightly with his right hand. "It's in here somewhere. Don't worry, I'll find it."

"I do worry, Dylan," she sighed, going over to

him. "You won't find your pulse by doing that. You're more likely to give yourself gangrene in your arm. Here, let me show you."

She stood close beside him and gently took his left hand. She turned it palm upward and pressed her fingertips lightly into the side of his wrist, into the small hollow at the base of his thumb.

"It's in there," she said. "Take it with your fingers, not your thumb. Your thumb has a pulse of its own and may confuse you. Watch the second hand of your watch and count how many beats there are to a minute. That's your pulse. Yours is a bit fast, isn't it?"

"It'll be up a bit now," he muttered, glancing at her face through her dusky hair.

She looked up. She was so close, her breath misted his glasses. She gave him an amused smile and dropped his wrist. "Get it back to normal before you start drawing," she said. "We don't want any false readings, do we?"

He watched her as she left the room, half smiling and wondering.

Here, in this place, she was so easy to be with — amiable and open and warm. Here there was unity between them, a rapport and an easiness that continually amazed and delighted him. But at school there was a distance between them. It was nothing she said or did: it was a subtle barrier, a slight lessening of her warmth, a withdrawal of a glance, an unspoken word that told him, "This far and no farther."

Her remoteness at school hurt him deeply, but

he accepted it because of all they shared here. He would suffer anything for this.

He sat on the floor by the sheets of paper and picked up one of the newly sharpened pencils. The sunlight poured across his bent head, glinting on the lenses of his glasses and shining on his fair hair. He closed his eyes, soaking in the peace of the attic. It was a place apart, separate, above the bustles and cares of everyday life. Here he belonged only to himself. And to Juniper.

He waited, almost dozing in the balmy golden light. For an hour and a half he waited, calm and at peace. He could smell the warm brown of the timbered walls and the heady fragrance of the flowers. Then something vibrated in his head like an unheard hum.

Juniper stepped over a low brick wall and stood looking at the demolition site. Only the chimney of the old factory remained, soaring above the chaos like the calm, incongruous pillar of some ancient temple. Huge piles of smashed concrete were everywhere, and crazily angled half-broken walls. She sat down on a flat slab of concrete and looked across the rubble. If she half closed her eyes, it looked almost like mountains, jagged and bare and savage. She checked the time. Four o'clock exactly.

She leaned her chin on her hands and gazed steadily at the scene in front of her.

Dylan's hand moved towards the paper, stopping on the edge, alert but relaxed and waiting.

Without moving again, he glanced at his watch. Four o'clock. He closed his eyes, hardly breathing, aware of a slight speeding up of his heart. Slowly, and with amazing clarity, the images poured across the darkness behind his eyes. It was like dreaming, only he was conscious. There were no vague, winging shapes this time: this time it was a tall structure, dark and solid against the sun, and a sloping, jagged form nearby.

Puzzled, he opened his eyes and drew the images. His pencil moved swiftly, without hesitation, drawing slanting and strangely angled lines. There was no order in the drawing, no pattern or regular shape, but there was a strength to the forms, something solid and real and three-dimensional. The lower half of the drawing became a mass of broken, disordered shapes, desolate and crumbling. But beyond them, towering dark and powerful, was a huge column. It was many times higher than the other shapes, yet it seemed to be a part of them. Heavy shadows slashed the tumultuous forms at its base, and something light played there, something small and fine and insubstantial. He couldn't make out what the fine things were; they moved and were fragile.

He stopped only long enough to take his pulse and found it was eighty-six. He made a note of it on the edge of the page and carried on drawing.

At last he put the pencil down and stared at the picture. "Holy cow — I've drawn a mountain!" he breathed. "A mountain of rocks, with a tower. Where's she gone — Tibet?"

He stood up slowly and hobbled over to the window. His legs were numb from sitting so long, he was sweating, and his whole body trembled. He felt as if he'd run a marathon. After a while he went downstairs and helped himself to a drink of tomato juice from the fridge. He looked at the kitchen clock. Six-fifteen. He'd been drawing non-stop for over two hours. No wonder he was exhausted.

He went out into the lounge and held his glass up to the da Vinci on the wall. "To your Virgin of the Rocks and to mine in Tibet," he said solemnly, and drank.

There was a chuckle behind him and he spun around, scarlet, the tomato juice a fine red moustache on his upper lip.

"Greetings, Leonardo," said Niall, smiling broadly. "That was an intriguing toast, I must say."

Dylan's blush deepened, and he didn't reply. Niall watched him, amused. "Are Marsha and Juniper both out?" he asked.

Dylan nodded and finished his drink. "Marsha's at aerobics, and Juniper's . . . ah . . ."

"In Tibet," said Niall gravely. "Well, it looks like you and I are the only ones left to get dinner." He stood up and went out into the kitchen. Dylan followed and watched as Niall raided the pantry, shelves, and fridge. "Salad it'll be," announced Niall, throwing a lettuce to Dylan. Dylan missed it, and the lettuce splattered on the floor. "Tossed salad, slightly bruised." Niall grinned. "Throw in anything you like. You'll find parsley and cress and a thousand other herbs in the garden. I'll do us some fish."

Dylan enjoyed working with Niall. There was something relaxed and easygoing about him; he wore no masks, made no judgements, and had no expectations of people. He was the most serene, gentle, and happy person Dylan had ever met. He talked easily with him, and they laughed often.

They had just finished preparing dinner when Marsha arrived home. She was carrying bags of groceries and had had a haircut.

"Mmmm . . . very nice," said Niall admiringly, turning her slowly around. He kissed her ears, nose, and neck. She pushed him away, laughing, and surveyed the chaotic kitchen benches and the scraps of vegetables and grated cheese all over the floor.

"This is a pleasant surprise," she said, her smile encompassing Dylan as well. "You've got dinner ready."

"Raw fish marinated in lemon juice, tomatoes, and tossed salad," announced Niall grandly. "A very tossed salad, actually, in Leonardo's own enthusiastic and inimitable style."

Dylan blushed, pleased. "I hope it's all right," he said. "Niall left it all up to me."

Marsha peered into the large pottery salad bowl and picked a canned shrimp out from between the lettuce and mint leaves. "Very artistic," she said approvingly. "And what's Juniper done towards all this? Given instructions?"

"She's not back yet," said Dylan. "She said to tell you she'd be late."

Marsha nodded and asked no questions.

But it was almost nine o'clock when Juniper got home, and even Dylan was beginning to be worried. She rushed in, bright-eyed and dishevelled, grabbed Dylan's arm, and went straight upstairs to the attic.

She knelt on the floor by Dylan's drawing and for a long time said nothing. He waited, silent and tense.

Slowly, she stood up. She went over to him and put her arms around his neck. "Dylan Pidgely, you're amazing," she whispered. "Absolutely amazing."

"I got it right again?" He was terrified, exultant, and overwhelmed by the nearness and warmth of her.

"Exactly," she laughed, hugging his neck. "Perfectly, incredibly right." She drew away from him and gazed at the picture on the floor. "It's the old factory out at Richmond," she explained. "They're demolishing it. The chimney's the only thing still standing. There are piles of toppled walls and bricks everywhere. You've even drawn the children playing on the rubble. There, see?"

She pointed to the slender, indistinct forms he had drawn lightly in the foreground. "They were playing in the sun," she said, "and were all lit up like fairy things. You've drawn the whole scene perfectly."

"But Richmond's thirty kilometres away!"

"That's why I was away so long. I had to catch two different buses. I missed the last connection coming home and had to hitch-hike."

"What'll Marsha say about that?"

"She's not going to know, is she? Don't look at me like that, Dylan. You did brilliantly today. Aren't you pleased?"

"Of course I am. It's not the drawing. It's you. Richmond's an awful place. Three girls were assaulted there last week. And you hitch-hiked."

She smiled and touched his cheek lightly with the back of her hand. "Do you worry about me, Leonardo?"

"Yes."

"But if anything terrible was going to happen in a place, I'd know, and I'd avoid it like the plague."

"Maybe it doesn't always work like that."

"It does for me."

He was silent for a long time, looking at her face. Slowly, he smiled.

"I suppose you're right," he said.

"I'm always right," she said.

And somehow he didn't doubt her.

9

High Dream

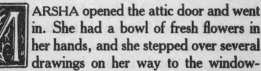ARSHA opened the attic door and went in. She had a bowl of fresh flowers in her hands, and she stepped over several drawings on her way to the window-seat. She put the flowers down, then bent to gather up the papers on the floor.

"They won't be using this place again if they don't leave it tidy," she said. She began placing the drawings on top of one another, casually, then stopped. Slowly, she spread the drawings out, putting them in order according to the dates and numbers written on them. For a long time she knelt there staring at them, astounded.

There were seven drawings now. There was the first, with its incredibly accurate recording of the new sculpture in the park. There was the portrait of Kingsley and the meaningless shadows and the stars. There was a stony, desolate landscape with a tower. The words under that were: "Third Result. Image sent: Richmond Factory, partly demolished." There were four more drawings, each one more intriguing than the last.

There was a large vague shape like an animal, with a strangely bumpy head almost as large as its body. The edges of the drawing were soft and indistinct, almost deliberately fuzzy. Underneath was written: "Fourth Result. Image sent: teddy-bear in shop window. D's pulse, 84. J's pulse, 89."

There was a picture of a children's playground, the merry-go-round and slides and swings easily recognisable. There was a shadowed, strongly drawn picture of what looked like a row of flat-topped, elongated houses close together and joined by narrow fences or chains. Under that Juniper had written: "Sixth Result. Image sent: train in railway yard. D's pulse, 79. J's pulse, 80." But the seventh drawing, and the last, was the most incredible of all.

It was a picture of a cathedral, its arching windows, spired tower, and angled roofs drawn with striking power and sensitivity. It was correct in every detail, the dimensions accurate, the perspective remarkable. As a work of art it was impressive; as a telepathically received image, it was almost unbelievable. For a few moments Marsha even suspected it had been left there deliberately for her to find as a hoax. She read the words on the foot of the page. "Seventh Result. Image sent: Wells

Cathedral. D's pulse, 92. J's pulse, 92. This is IT."

The drawing slipped from Marsha's hands, but she made no move to pick it up. Her face was white. Wells Cathedral was in Britain, half a world away. What was Juniper doing? Marsha's thoughts were a jumble, a tumult of fear and amazement and disbelief.

From somewhere distant in the house came the faint sound of a flute, beautifully played. The sounds wove upwards along the wooden stairways and coloured light, mellow and lingering. They brought harmony to Marsha's mind and a kind of peace. She smiled, bending to pick up the drawing. She put it on the floor with the others, then went downstairs to see Niall.

"Good morning, lovely light of my soul," he said, putting down his flute. "I've come to invite you to a day of sunlight and pure joy in my palace by the willows."

She returned his smile but curled into a chair opposite him, tense, saying nothing. He picked up his flute and played again, a soft and haunting ancient melody that was meant to soothe but didn't.

"Not medieval music, please," she said. Then she covered her face with her hands. "Niall, I don't know what to do. Juniper and Dylan are doing something amazing, and I don't know where it's leading them. I don't think they know themselves. I don't know what to do."

He went over and crouched in front of her and

took her hands down from her face, gently. "You could start by telling me about it," he said.

"It's probably best if you come and see for yourself," she replied.

Upstairs, Niall knelt on the floor in front of the drawings, while Marsha explained briefly how they were done. He touched the drawings, amazed and half smiling. "The little witch," he murmured. "No wonder she always wins at cards. She *is* clairvoyant."

"Don't call her a witch."

"I'm sorry, love. I meant it only lightly. They're not doing anything wrong, you know. Even you and I have a sixth sense about each other, remember: that intuitive understanding when the other is unhappy or in pain; the contact when it's most needed; the gift that's perfectly timed for a special need."

He stood up and cupped her face in his hands and kissed her. "Maybe we should ask them to give us a few lessons," he grinned. "Then I could blow a sweet message straight into your mind without ever having to get on my bike and go all the way to the phone box."

She laughed in spite of her fears. "It's not funny, Niall. This is serious."

"I know it is. Those two could make a fortune if they went into show business."

"Niall!"

"I'm sorry. But I think you're getting it a bit out of perspective."

"What about Wells Cathedral, then? That's not

even in this hemisphere. So how did she send that to him?"

"Postcard maybe?" He laughed softly. "All right, I'll be serious. Maybe she sent him a picture out of a book."

"Of course! Her medieval book!"

Marsha ran out of the attic, down several short flights of stairs, and across a small landing to Juniper's room. She crouched in front of Juniper's bookshelves.

"It's not here," she said, disappointed. "It's a big book on medieval architecture. Her grandparents gave it to her for her eighth birthday. She's always loved it."

"It's influenced her whole life!" Niall remarked, looking around. "There's medieval stuff everywhere! She's even got straw on the floor!"

"We had to go all the way to a farm for that," smiled Marsha. "Our humble grass clippings weren't good enough. She never vacuums in here, of course. She sweeps it all up carefully, takes it outside, and winnows the dust out of it. The neighbours must think we keep donkeys."

"What's the smell in here? Mint?"

"Mint and marjoram. They're the strewing herbs in the straw."

"Where did she get all this stuff? It's like a museum in here."

"She's gleaned it over the years, by fair means or foul. Mainly foul, I suspect," said Marsha. "A lot of it came from second-hand shops. The castle tapestry she wheedled off her grandmother. The stained glass window is from a church that burned down a few years ago. She restored it herself."

"What's that shelf for?" asked Niall, looking at a beautifully hand-carved shelf in the centre of a wall, surrounded by a wreath of dried flowers. The shelf was empty but obviously special.

"That shelf is waiting for a genuine fifteenth-century chalice," said Marsha. "A friend of hers owns it. He's a professor of medieval history and an author. He's promised to leave it to her in his will."

"I hope he's old for her sake."

"He is. He's ninety. She predicts she'll have the chalice by the time she's twenty-five. I guess she doesn't have to be clairvoyant to be right about that. Ah — there's the book!"

There was an antique chest against the wall beside the bed, and the book was lying in the centre of it, between a candle and a white porcelain dove. Marsha sat on the edge of the bed, the book across her knees. There was a black velvet ribbon marking a place, and that was where she opened it.

It was Wells Cathedral, exactly as Dylan had drawn it.

At the bottom of the page, in pencil, Juniper had written a date and the words: "The last material image sent. From now on, we fly."

10

The Dream Realised

YLAN and Juniper burst through the front doorway, laughing and breathless, and raced into the kitchen. Dylan wrenched open the fridge door, looking for something to drink.

"Any gingerbeer, Marsha?" he called to the house in general.

"None cold," called Marsha from the lounge. "You'll have to have apple juice."

Juniper sniffed the carrot cake on the bench and ran her finger along the icing on the edge.

Marsha called out sharply, "Get your fingers out of that cake, Juniper. It's for dessert."

Juniper gave Dylan a sly smile and licked her finger. "I think she's clairvoyant, too," she said.

"No, I'm not," said Marsha, coming into the

kitchen. "I know you too well, that's all. You're late today."

"I had a detention," said Dylan from deep in the pantry. "Juniper waited for me. Haven't you got any biscuits?"

"No," said Marsha. Then she realised what he'd said. "*You* had a detention, Dylan Pidgely?"

He came out of the pantry, an apple in each hand, and grinned at her. "My first," he said. "I got into trouble in Music."

Juniper tried to catch his eye, but he was too busy eating. "We were listening to music," he explained to Marsha. "It was Rimsky-Korsakov's bumblebee thing — "

"*The Flight of the Bumblebee?*" said Niall helpfully, coming into the kitchen.

Dylan nodded. "Yes. That buzzy one. Anyway, we were all listening quietly, and we were supposed to be imagining the bees. Then I got this picture of a whole lot of little hippos in pink aeroplanes. They were — " He started to laugh and choked on his apple. Juniper thumped him on the back, giggling.

Dylan got himself under control and went on: "They were buzzing around in these little pink planes with purple hearts on them, in perfect time to the music, and then they popped out in these little rainbow parachutes — " He collapsed over the bench, chortling uncontrollably. "And then — then I laughed so much I had to leave the room. They were so cute!"

Juniper leaned on him, and they both collapsed in a heap on the floor, hooting with laughter.

Bewildered, Niall crouched in front of them and peered into their faces. They blinked at him, chuckling helplessly, their eyes streaming.

"Have you been smoking?" Niall asked quietly.

Dylan shook his head emphatically. "No. Just watching hippos."

Niall stood up, looked at Marsha, and shrugged. "Just a case of teenage temporary insanity, I think," he said.

But Marsha frowned and went into the lounge. "You know why he saw hippos, don't you?" she said. "She gave them to him."

"I suppose you're right," he said with a sudden smile. "Her talent could be quite useful in school."

"Exactly. And it's not funny."

"You think she'd give him the answers in exams, that sort of thing?"

"I don't know. She has the ability. If she can send him a whole herd of hippos in full flight, she can send him anything."

Niall went over to the window and looked out at the garden, his back to Marsha. But she could see his shoulders shaking with mirth. She went over and stood beside him. "It's not funny, Niall," she murmured.

"You keep saying that," he chuckled. "I'm sorry, love, but I don't agree. I think it's hilarious. I wish she'd show them to me."

*   *   *

75

In the attic, Juniper took Dylan's second apple out of his hand and placed it on the windowseat. "No more eating," she said. "This doesn't work well if you've got a full stomach. And I hope you're not eating red meat at home. I'm sure that messes up telepathic energies. You're not, are you?"

"I wouldn't dare," he said. "You'd probably know and send me images of slaughtered beasts to put me off."

She sat in front of him, her face suddenly grave. "Dylan? Remember that cathedral you drew? The last time?"

"How could I forget it? Drawing that was the happiest thing I've ever done in my life."

"Well, think of that as paddling around in the mud. Today we're going to fly."

He blinked, astounded. "Like the hippos?"

She sighed. "Dylan, please forget the hippos. I'm beginning to wish I'd never made them. If you start laughing again, I'll thump you. Dylan! Now, listen. I'm sending you something different this time. I don't even know if you'll be able to draw it. If you receive an impression you can't draw, please write it down. Just a word, something to help you recall it later. Do you understand?"

"Yes, Miss Golding."

She sighed. "I just want you to be very careful this time."

"What do you think I do while you're out there hitch-hiking around — soak up a bottle of wine and draw blindfolded?"

"Point taken," she said. "I'm sure you'll do beautifully."

"Thank you."

"You're welcome." She looked at her watch. "It's nearly half past five. I'll start sending an image at a quarter to six."

His eyebrows rose. "You're not leaving yourself much travelling time today," he observed. "Going on your broomstick?"

She shot him a withering look. "I didn't mean that kind of flying," she said, and went out.

She went noisily downstairs and along the passage to the front door. She opened it, then slammed it closed again. Soundlessly she took off her shoes and crept back up the stairs to her room. Quietly she went in and closed the door behind her. She sat on the bed, cross-legged, took off her watch, and put it on the quilt in front of her. For a long time she looked around at her beloved medieval things, the pictures and tapestries and brass rubbings. Then she relaxed, breathing deeply, her hands palm uppermost on her knees. She closed her eyes.

Dylan waited, calm and relaxed and alert. He felt his heart begin to quicken, and he closed his eyes, expectant and ready.

He had a feeling of darkness and of ancient things, of being in a place outside his own time. It was an awesome feeling, and at first it alarmed him. There were no images; just this deep stillness and a sense of another reality. He waited, breathing shallowly, and looked along the dark corridors of his mind.

Out of the dimness, like a film appearing slowly on a screen, he saw a street. It was dark at first, rough and cobbled, and again came the feeling of great antiquity. Fascinated, he explored the street. He was no longer afraid — just excited and filled with a tremendous wonder. It was like seeing a movie, only he was inside it, not outside observing; it was an experience, an encounter with something three-dimensional and real.

He walked down the street and came to a wall on his right. It was high, and he couldn't see over it. The stones seemed very old. He followed the wall for a short distance and came to a house. He glanced up, surprised. The house wasn't large, though it appeared to have three stories. The plastered stone walls were pale and glimmering. The door off the street was low and very old. The windows, too, were low, edged with heavy wooden beams and covered with narrow wooden shutters. There was no glass. One of the shutters was slightly open, but he could see only darkness inside.

The second story jutted out, and he could see the protruding ends of the great floor beams. He could almost reach them with his hand. Above the beams was another window, heavily surrounded in wood and standing out slightly from the wall. The gabled roof above was sharply pitched and leaning out and gave the house a feeling of crookedness about to topple.

Dylan stepped back from the house, smiling, enthralled. He knew he was in a street in medieval England, yet somehow it felt familiar, comfortable and known.

Suddenly he remembered he should be drawing. He opened his eyes and picked up the pencil. The dim street, the impression of great age, the oddly toppling house, remained with him, vivid and utterly real. He began drawing quickly, joyful and inspired. He didn't have to close his eyes to see what he needed to see; it was within him, all around him, a place and a time he experienced and knew with all of his being.

He was drawing the steps and the doorway when he noticed with a shock that a girl was standing there. She had a basket containing plants and berries. Her back was to him, but she was looking over her shoulder, alert, almost as if she were aware of him. He could smell a dewy, earthy smell and the wild, sweet odour of freshly gathered herbs. Swiftly, he drew her; the woven texture of her ankle-length skirt and the tattered leather of her loose shoes. He drew her white apron and the bow at the back where it tied. He drew the strange little white cap she wore and her smooth pale hair falling in thick braids from underneath. He drew the faint gleam of her half-turned face, her softly pointed chin, wide fine cheekbones, and her vivid shining eye.

He finished the house, shading in the details of the timbered beams and the rough texture of the wood. He drew the edges of the tiles around the eaves and the deeper blackness inside the shuttered windows. With the tip of his little finger he polished the berries in the girl's basket and with charcoal deepened the shadow where her foot rested on the step.

Then he put down his pencil and rested his head in his hands. Suddenly he took hold of his wrist, his eyes on his watch, and took his pulse. It was a hundred and five.

He sighed and relaxed, looking at the drawing in front of him.

It was magnificent. The house was exactly as he had experienced it, solid and crazily tilted and charming. The shadows were deep and dim with age, and the street had no end.

And the fair girl who stood in the doorway and almost smiled had a haunting, elfin face.

11

A Deepening
of Dylan's Troubles

HE phone rang, loud and insistent, and Dylan threw down his pen. "Robyn?" he yelled, angrily. "Barbie? Will someone answer that?"

No one did, and he swore and went down the passage to the kitchen.

"Hello," he snapped into the mouthpiece.

"No need to answer the phone in that tone of voice," said his father.

"Well, I'm trying to do my homework."

"My humble apologies," said Tom. "I didn't mean to interrupt the great intellectual effort of the century. Is your mother there?"

"No."

"When she gets in, tell her I'll be home late tonight."

"I thought you were taking her to the movies.

It's that one about Chopin that she wanted to see, with all the piano stuff in it."

"Something's cropped up. I can't go."

"Why? I thought you were out building that aviary."

"I am. But things have got a bit complicated. Explain to your mother for me?"

What could be complicated about a birdcage, Dylan thought. Electronic ferret alarms? Aloud he said, "What shall I tell her?"

"Anything you like. See you later."

"Dad?"

But Tom had hung up. Dylan shrugged and went back to his homework. It was an essay on energy conservation, and he was having difficulty with it. He envied Juniper, whose essay had been written in under an hour, and for which she would get the usual brilliant mark. He picked up his pen and gnawed the end of it, thinking.

A while later he heard his mother come home and remembered, guiltily, that he was supposed to be keeping an eye on the twins. But he heard them talking to their mother in the kitchen, so he knew they must have survived whatever mutinous activities they'd been indulging in. He wrote for another ten minutes, then heard his mother call.

"Dylan? Will you get the washing in for me? It looks like it's going to rain. And will you run a bath for the twins?"

"Why don't we just stand the little beggars out in the rain and squirt detergent on them?" he muttered, going outside. He got the washing off the line, dumped it in the laundry, and started running the bath. It was partly full when he remembered the phone call from his father. He went into the kitchen.

"Mum? Dad phoned before. He's going to be a bit late."

Kathy looked up from the fried rissoles. "He's remembered we're going to the movies, hasn't he? He promised weeks ago we'd go to this one. I've got the tickets." She smiled and looked suddenly different, softer and almost younger. "This is the first time your father's taken me out since we've been here, Dylan. Give me a hand to mash the potatoes, will you? I hope he's not going to be too late. His dinner'll get cold."

Dylan took the saucepan off the stove and drained the water out. The steam burnt his hand, and he dropped the pot on the bench.

"Dad can't take you out, Mum," he said. "That's what he was ringing for. He's . . . he's still doing that job, I think."

"For the Honeyburn woman?"

"I don't know. He said he was sorry."

Kathy left the stove and went and sat heavily in one of the dining chairs, her back to her son. He finished mashing the potatoes and put them back on the stove to keep warm. He went and stood beside his mother.

"He said he was sorry, Mum."

To his horror, he realised she was crying. His first impulse was to run and leave her to it. He put his hand on her shoulder, awkwardly. "I'm sorry,

Mum. Maybe he can take you tomorrow night."

"Tonight's the last night."

"Maybe it'll come back another time. They always bring films back."

"Dish dinner for the twins, will you?"

"Weren't they going to have a b — "

At that moment there was a scream from the other end of the house.

"MUM! THERE'S WATER EVERY-WHERE!"

Dylan raced out into the passage. Water seeped towards him across the carpet, all the way along the passage; it was trickling into the bedrooms and was already halfway across the carpet in the lounge. He splashed across the warm tide and turned off the bath taps. He leaned over the bath, his eyes closed, his feet in four centimetres of water, and said a word never before spoken in his home.

The twins, watching from the doorway, gasped and then giggled.

"Jimmy Bryan got sent to the headmaster for saying that," said Robyn, impressed.

Dylan looked at them. His face was white. "Go and get me a mop and bucket from the laundry," he said.

They galloped off, shrieking and giggling, their feet making squelching sounds all down the passage. Dylan pulled some towels from the bathroom cupboard and dropped them onto the lake on the floor. He plunged his arm into the water in the bath and, with difficulty, extracted the plug. Then despairingly, he began wringing the wet towels into the emptying bath.

The twins arrived, grinning, and elbowed their way into the narrow bathroom.

"Scoop up as much water as you can," said Dylan. "I'll use the mop. No — don't play in it! Look, like this. And tip it into the bath, not over each other. And don't make waves in it — it'll only go out over more of the carpet. What's Mum doing?"

"She's gone out," said Barbara, flinging half a bucket of water roughly in the direction of the bath. She missed and poured it all over Dylan's bent back. He stood up and glared at her, then wrenched the bucket out of her hands.

"And there's something on fire on the stove," she added casually.

Dylan dropped the bucket and raced into the kitchen. Smoke was billowing from the saucepan of mashed potatoes. He hadn't turned the hot plate down. And the rissoles were black. He filled the saucepan with water and left the sizzling, revolting mess in the sink. He rescued the rissoles and turned the stove off, then went back to the bathroom.

The twins had stripped off and were squatting in the water, scooping it up into tiny doll's cups and tipping it slowly into the bath. They were smothered with soap, and their curly heads glistened with shampoo.

"We're having a bath at the same time," explained Barbara cheerfully, "so we don't waste hot water. Mummy says we're not allowed to waste hot water because of the power bill."

Dylan sighed and picked up one of the dripping towels.

It was two-fifteen in the morning when he dropped the last dirty towel into the washing machine. He got the heater out of the garage and put it on in the lounge to start drying out the carpet. He opened all the windows and hoped the breeze would help. The whole house stank of burnt potato, wet carpet, and warm rubber underlay. The smell was almost worse than the damage.

He looked into the twins' bedroom. They were sound asleep, their toys, clothes, and books piled high onto the ends of their beds, clear of the damp floor. He looked into his parents' room. The bed was untouched. His mother hadn't come back yet, and his father was still out.

Dylan went into his own room, padded wearily across the wet carpet, and peeled off his damp clothes. He should have a shower but he was too tired. Pulling on his pyjamas, he went out to the kitchen, cleared a space on the bench, and made himself a peanut butter sandwich. He ignored the disgusting saucepan and the greasy dishes on the table. The twins had wrapped the burnt rissoles in bread, plastered them with tomato sauce, and eaten them while they watched television, perched on chairs above the stained carpet. They had thoroughly enjoyed themselves; it was the most exciting time they'd had since the night Dad came home drunk.

Dylan took the first bite of his sandwich and stopped, listening. There was a furtive noise at the other end of the house.

"Is that you, Mum?" he called, going to the door and peering down the passage. The house was in darkness. All he could see was the red glow from the heater in the lounge.

Then a light flicked on and his father stood there, looking startled and uneasy. "What's going on, Dylan? What's that awful smell? And where's your mother?"

Dylan took another bite of his sandwich. "I don't know, Dad. She went. We had a flood. It was my fault. She left in the middle of it."

Tom put his hand against the wall, supporting himself. He could hardly speak. "She's left home? Did she leave a note?"

"No, Dad. Not left home. Just walked out. For the evening, I guess. I thought she must have gone to the movies by herself. I'm sorry about the carpet. I cleaned up as much as I could. I've got the heater on in the lounge, drying it out."

"Didn't she say where she was going?"

"No."

"Oh, Dylan. What a mess. What an awful mess." Tom went into the lounge and sat there in the darkness, his head in his hands. The light from the heater glowed dimly on his bald patch, and Dylan felt a sudden deep tenderness for him.

"I'm sorry, Dad," he murmured. "If we have to buy a new carpet, I'll get a job at the supermarket or something to help pay for it."

"I'm not talking about the carpet, Dylan. I don't care about the carpet. It's us. Me and your mum."

Dylan threw the rest of his sandwich into the papers in the fireplace and stood miserably in the doorway. "I'm going to bed now, Dad, if you don't mind. I'm beat."

He turned and went into his room, turned on the light, and closed the door. He stood leaning against it, breathing hard, trying not to think, trying desperately not to feel.

After a while he went over to his desk and the unfinished homework. From between the scrawled notes he drew out a small drawing. It was a portrait of Juniper, done from memory. He had captured her perfectly. Her eyes were solemn and shadowed, her lips sultry and slightly curved. It was the way she sometimes looked; veiled, remote, mysterious, and utterly beautiful.

He propped the portrait up against his pile of textbooks, where he could see it, and climbed into bed. For a long time he lay there, his hands linked behind his head, looking at her face.

"Good night, Juniper," he said softly, half wondering whether she would hear. "You know, you're the only good thing in my life."

Then he turned over towards the wall and went to sleep.

12

Time-stream

HEY were eating breakfast when Kathy arrived home. They heard her come in the front door and go into the bathroom.

Tom put down his coffee. "You kids stay here," he said. "Dylan, I don't want your Mum and I to be disturbed. You see the twins off to school. Make sure they've got their lunches and their swimming gear."

He went out, closing the door between the kitchen and the passage.

Robyn went on eating, gravely. "I bet she gets a hiding," she said.

"Don't be stupid," said Dylan.

"We'd get a hiding if we stayed out all night," remarked Barbara. She thought for a few moments, then grinned impishly at her sister. "We could do that, you know. We could take some sandwiches and some blankets and our dolls and teddybears and dressing gowns, and we could run away and sleep outside."

"In the dark?" asked Robyn, round-eyed.

" 'Course. We could sleep in that little Hansel and Gretel house in the playground."

"It'd be scary," said Robyn doubtfully.

"And crowded," said Dylan. "By the time you got in there with all your gear, plus Hansel and Gretel and the witch, you'd all be squashed."

"The witch wouldn't be there," said Barbara, poking out her tongue.

They heard their mother's voice in the bathroom, raised, shouting through the closed door. She sounded as if she were crying. Dylan turned the radio on, and Barbara turned it off. "I want to hear," she said.

"Well, you're not." Dylan turned it on again.

They heard their father shouting and Kathy shrieking back. Dylan turned the radio up. He got up from the table and began doing the dishes. As he filled the sink, he noticed that his hands were shaking. He felt ridiculously like crying.

Robyn was crying, whimpering softly like a frightened animal. The shouting went on, their mother sounding high and hysterical. Then Barbara started to sob. Dylan left the sink and tried to comfort them, but they squirmed away from his unfamiliar embrace, howling. So he left them to their noisy grief and finished cleaning up the kitchen. He had to do last night's messy dinner things as well. By the time he'd finished, the twins had worn themselves out. They were sitting on the back step with their schoolbags, giving long, quivering sighs and looking like a pair of blotchy goblins.

Dylan went down to his room, doing his best to ignore the angry shouting from his parents' room, and threw his unfinished homework into his bag. He combed his hair and pretended not to notice how pale he looked. His hands were still shaking and his breakfast was churning in his stomach. He went outside and got his bike, then called to the twins. He walked with them down the footpath to the busy intersection, where they were to go one way and he the other.

"I'll see you after school," he said, wishing they looked happier. "Cross the roads carefully, won't you?"

"Will Mummy be home after school?" asked Robyn in a small voice.

"Of course she will. 'Bye."

The girls shuffled off, and he had the crazy impulse to call them back and hug them. Instead, he watched until they disappeared around the next corner.

Dylan sighed and looked at his watch. Seven minutes past nine. He was going to have to walk in late for English and hand in a half-finished essay. And the day had hardly started yet.

*　　*　　*

Juniper gave Dylan a glass of gingerbeer and sat beside him on the sofa. Smiling sympathetically, she touched her glass to his.

"To a better day tomorrow," she said.

"It has to be better," he sighed. "It can't possibly be worse."

"Cheer up, Leonardo. You're safe here. No one's going to yell at you for being late and not finishing your homework; no one's going to laugh if you fall asleep in your chair; no one's going to tease you; and, definitely, no one's going to let you anywhere near water. Here, you're Leonardo — visionary and artist, and my welcome friend. So where's your smile?"

He gave it, and she cheered loudly. "The first smile of the day!" she cried triumphantly. "The first sign of celebration and life! Ah, 'tis good for my soul, to see thy sunny face!"

"Shakespeare?" he asked, chuckling, spilling his drink on his trousers.

"No. Better than him. Me." She flashed a brilliant smile. "You really are expert at spilling things, aren't you, Dylan Pidgely?"

"I get lots of practise," he said.

She went off and got a cloth for him.

"I'm glad you don't work in pen and ink," she remarked, coming back. "The results would be more than I could bear."

"Actually, I was going to ask if I could try watercolours," he said, mopping at his trousers. "But maybe I won't."

"Leonardo," she said generously, "you want

watercolours, you can have watercolours. You can have oilpaints if you want them. You can have chalks, crayons, pastels, tempera, palette knives, canvases, clay, bronze, marble, the ceiling of the Sistine Chapel. Anything! Anything, except pen and ink."

He shook his head, laughing. "Watercolours would be nice."

"I have some," she said. "They're in my chamber, where I sleep. Wait here."

She returned a short while later, a wooden box in her hands, and they went up to the attic. She crouched on the floor beside him and opened the lid. Together they spread out the paints. There were over thirty tubes of high-quality watercolours and seven sable-hair brushes of varying thicknesses.

Dylan was ecstatic. "I've always wanted to use paints like these," he breathed, turning a crimson tube over and over in his hand. "We could never afford them."

"My grandmother gave them to me," said Juniper. "She's always giving us money and lovely things. She's very wealthy and generous with it. She paid off the mortgage on this house for Marsha."

"You're lucky," he said with a grin.

"Will you paint while I send you the image?" she asked. "Or will you just draw it then and paint it later?"

"I'll draw it the way I usually do," he said, "and make notes of the colours. I'll do all the shading with a pencil, the same as before. Then I'll spray the whole drawing with a fixative to stop it from smudging. Then I'll paint it, but only lightly, leaving the pencil drawing showing through. It'll look like a softly coloured photograph. I've seen the effect in a book. It's great."

She stood up, eager and excited. "We'll get on with it, then."

He stood with her, the tube of paint still in his hands, his head bent. "Juniper? What did you actually do when you sent that last image — the medieval one? Was it really just your imagination?"

For a full minute she stood there, looking at him with a strange expression on her face, saying nothing. She reminded him of the twins when they were caught doing something forbidden and they didn't know whether to lie about it, confess, or flee.

"I think I'd better explain," Juniper said at last, sitting down again.

He sat with her on the windowseat, their heads and shoulders bathed in yellow afternoon sun. For a while Juniper was silent, thinking, staring at her hands. They were turned palm upwards, peacefully, as though offering a gift. They were filled with light.

"I think I do only imagine everything," she said. "But I'm not sure. What I see when I meditate has a feeling of surprise about it, as if it comes to me from outside. I didn't exactly sit down the other day with the idea of imagining a medieval street and a house and a girl with a basket of herbs and berries. I discovered them as I was going along. Can you understand?"

"Yes. That's exactly the way I felt."

"Of course. Well, it's the same for me. The only thing I deliberately think of is a feeling for medieval things. Where the images come from, I don't really know. It's as if I set sail in a certain direction, but then I have to go where the wind blows me, or where the current goes, or to where I'm drawn."

"I can understand that," he said. "But where could the images come from? They must come from somewhere. Or someone."

"I think it may be something to do with time, Dylan. There's a theory that time isn't the way we think it is — that it isn't chronological and divided neatly into past, present, and future. Maybe there's just an eternal Now, real and ever-moving, where all time occurs simultaneously. And this Now can be travelled through, forwards or backwards, and the people and places in it can be sometimes seen."

"Are you saying that you travel through time?" asked Dylan, incredulous. "That the street we saw, and the house and the girl, are all real?"

"I don't know. It's a theory. I've read about it in several books. Einstein had ideas about it; so did Carl Jung. Lots of ancient cultures believed in it, and that's why, for some people, tribal lands and traditions and ancestors are so important: they never really ceased to exist. Maybe that's what Christ was talking about when He called Himself the 'I am,' and Alpha and Omega, the Beginning and the End. It's a whole new concept of time. Well, not new: old, really. It's as if there is no time. I don't really understand it all, Dylan. I just know that it explains some of the things I've experienced."

She hesitated, and he looked into her face, his own face bewildered and amazed. "Go on," he said. "I'm with you."

She took a deep breath and went on.

"When I was six years old, I went to see an old man I know, a professor of medieval history. He had a fifteenth-century wine chalice and he let me hold it. I can't explain how I felt, Dylan; I felt homesick. Terribly homesick. I wanted something, and I didn't know what. It was a longing, an almost physical hunger and pain, and I didn't know what to do about it. At the same time I was happy — happier than I'd ever been in my whole life. It was like coming home and longing for my home all at once. It was like being suddenly caught up into something beyond myself, something joyful and huge and holy. I cried and cried while I held that chalice, and I couldn't stop.

"Soon after that, I had a dream. I saw a girl my own age, wearing a long brown dress with a high waist and a very full skirt. She wore a plain white cap on her head, tied under her chin. Her hair was long and gold and waved as if it had been plaited, and her eyes were blue. I'll never forget her eyes.

"She was playing with a white dove. It seemed big in her arms, and it amazed me because it didn't try to fly away. It stayed there, and she stroked it and smoothed its feathers, and it wasn't afraid. It just cooed softly — you know how doves do — and she talked to it and laughed. Then it flew up onto her shoulder, and someone came and took her hand and led her away. I didn't really see the other person; only her.

"And it wasn't really a dream, Dylan. I was awake and playing under a hedge in the sun."

Dylan didn't say anything for a while; he didn't look at Juniper, and he didn't move. Then he asked: "Did you ever see her again?"

"Yes. I think it was her the other day, standing in the doorway. But she was older then. I must have seen her at a different place in Now."

Dylan looked at her sharply, then he shook his head. "No. No, I can't accept all that," he said. "I think you imagined it. All of it. Even her. Especially her."

"Did you imagine her?" she asked.

He fell silent, his hands clenched on his thighs, his glasses misted over. He took them off and polished them slowly on his sleeve. "I don't know," he said. "I'll have to think about it."

He put his glasses back on and looked at her. "That's why you wanted to do this image transfer thing, isn't it, Juniper? You weren't really interested in sculptures and chimneys and teddybears in shop windows. What you really wanted was someone to draw these other places you see."

"Do you mind?"

"Not really. But you could have told me."

"I just have, and you can hardly take it in. If I'd told you all this a month ago, you'd have said I was mad."

He smiled. "You're not mad," he murmured. "I'm not sure what you are, Juniper. A mystic, maybe. A pilgrim in untrod ways."

"Very poetic, Leonardo," she grinned. "And if I'm a pilgrim, so are you. And it's time we made some progress." She hesitated, seeing his face. "Are you worried about this, Dylan?"

"A bit. Are you?"

"Like you, just a bit. If this is real, and I'm not just imagining it all, there must be people who have done it before and proper ways of doing it. There must be — well — rules, I suppose. Safety rules for telepathic travellers. I wish I knew someone else who'd done it."

"Couldn't you find out?"

"I could put an ad in the paper, I suppose. 'Wanted: Similar soul who's travelled in time. Meet me outside the Roman Senate on the ides of March. Preferably when Brutus isn't around.' "

Dylan laughed. "You're crazy."

"I know. If I'd lived in medieval times, I wouldn't have been called a pilgrim and been let off so lightly. I'd have been burned as a witch."

She turned to leave the room, but he called her back. "Juniper? Did you mean that?"

"About Brutus?" she asked. "No. He wouldn't stab me, anyway. He was after Caesar."

"Not him. You. About you being burnt as a witch."

She came back and sat on the windowseat, regarding him thoughtfully.

"Dylan, a woman could be suspected of witchcraft just because she owned a broomstick and grew herbs. It was dangerous in those days to be different. And being clever with medicines, or independent, or clairvoyant, was definitely different. It was the difference between being harmless and being a witch."

Dylan was not sure she was serious. "They had trials for witches, didn't they?" he said. "Even a lawyer with half a brain could tell that growing parsley doesn't make someone a witch. God, they'd have killed off half the women in England!"

"They almost did," she said.

She stood up and turned away from him, her face towards the window and the shining afternoon. "Medieval trials weren't anything to do with logic," she murmured. "They had a trial by cold water, called floating a witch. The priests said special prayers over a river and blessed the waters, then the person accused of witchcraft was bound hand and foot and thrown in. If she drowned, it meant the river accepted her, and she was innocent. If she survived, the river was rejecting her because she was guilty, so she was tortured and burnt."

For a while neither of them said anything. Dylan sensed a deep uneasiness in her and a fear, which he couldn't understand. He went over to her and gently stroked her hair. "Cheer up, sweet witch," he said lightly. "We're five centuries too late for the hot stuff."

She turned her head and looked at him, her face grave and strangely remote. "It's not the fire I'm afraid of," she said. Then she smiled, suddenly bright again, and glanced at her watch. "You'd better sharpen your pencils, Leonardo. I'll see you somewhere in the fifteenth century at five o'clock."

She went out, and Dylan sat on the floor by the sheets of drawing paper and waited.

13

Somewhere
in the Fifteenth Century

HE darkness was the most intense Juniper had ever known. She could not see her hand if she lifted it to her face; she could hear nothing; feel nothing. She knew only that she was standing, and that there was a vast space all around. Then, slowly, sounds came to her from far, far away: the deep tones of men's voices singing and the brighter tones of a flute or pipes. Then came women's voices joining in the song and the strumming of music from a mandolin. The sounds came gradually nearer, dissolving sometimes into laughter and then following the jaunty tune of the pipes again.

Juniper felt her hair move, as if a small breeze blew; yet she felt no coolness of air on her face. She smelled damp earth and grass and a sweet, heady fragrance of honeysuckle. She became aware that she was standing in long, wet grass, and that there were leaves and twigs against her back; yet she didn't feel these things but only knew they were there. The air lightened, became a glimmering, misty grey, and she saw that she was in a strange countryside close beside a wild hedge. A dirt road ran nearby, indistinct in the early dawn. The mist cleared, and the voices came closer, some laughing and chattering, some still singing. There was a deep undertone like a rumbling of wheels, and the occasional snorting of beasts.

The pipes stopped, and a young man's voice rose above all the others, sounding amused but authoritative. They all laughed at what he said, and the sound rang in the frosty air.

Juniper saw a crowd of people walking along the road towards her, the women's dresses gauzy white, the men's robes livid and deep against the morning grey. She shrank back into the shadows of the hedge and watched them pass.

There were about thirty people altogether, all young men and women. Many of them were obviously in pairs, arms about each other's shoulders and waists; some of the single men ran after the girls, calling soft endearments, and were laughingly pushed away. Everyone carried branches of green leaves and wild flowers, and many girls had flowers in their hair. The men wore thick, coloured stockings and short tunics with wide, flowing sleeves. All wore soft shoes with pointed toes, and Juniper noticed that they wore short knives at their belts, and some had soft draw-string purses. The women's dresses were long and simple. Some had put up their hair, but the dancing of the night, the walk along wild hedgerows, and the gathering of branches and flowers had caused long strands to tumble down.

Behind them came a team of oxen pulling a long wooden hay-cart. The cart was covered with leaves and bore a long maypole, richly decorated with flowers, herbs, banners, and long coloured ribbons. The ribbons fluttered against the deep leaves and the wood of the cart, streaming brilliant red and gold and blue against the dark. The flowers glowed softly, as pale and glimmering as the faces of the young men and women.

The oxen, too, were decorated, their horns crowned with blossoms and soft branches. Their warm breath misted on the still morning air, and they snorted and puffed as they pulled the heavy cart along the road. The man with the mandolin started playing again, and the crowd began singing.

No one noticed Juniper. They all passed by, their song punctuated often by laughter and ribald jokes. Some of them danced in time to the song, the pale dresses of the women swaying softly above the shadows on the road. They all passed by and were soon gone except for the last couple, walking slowly, their arms entwined.

They lagged behind, and the man drew the woman off the road and into the shadows by Juniper, so close that she could smell the wild rosemary and flowers in the girl's hair and the pungent odour of the green branches she carried.

103

"Tarry a while, dear heart," the man murmured, drawing the girl close. She moved easily against him, laughing, her voice breathless from the singing and the walk. Her back was to Juniper, and Juniper could see that her hair was a light, shining gold, falling straight almost to her knees and bound by a white ribbon wound around it.

They kissed, and there were whistles and catcalls from their friends along the road.

"Leave the maid alone, Edmund!" a man called jokingly. "She's not thy wife till Whitsun week."

Edmund laughed quietly and stopped kissing her, but they didn't immediately return to the road. He held her for a few moments more, and she leaned against him with her head on his shoulder, while he stroked her hair with his long, pale fingers and threaded in a sprig of rosemary where it had fallen out. For a moment he looked almost directly at Juniper, but his eyes retained their smiling, dreaming look and never focused on her face. She watched him, unmoving, not daring to breathe.

He was so close she could see the soft grey fur on his deep blue coat, and every hollow and line on his face. His was an unusual face, narrow and finely boned, the mouth well formed and the chin slightly cleft. His eyes were heavy-lidded, and the irises were a golden green. His hair was light brown and shoulder-length, and softly curled. He was about seventeen.

He whispered something to the girl, and she lifted her head and ran her hand lightly down his cheek. Juniper noticed that she wore a gold ring with a small purple stone. She was almost sure it was the same girl who had stood in the doorway with the basket of herbs on her arm, and she wished desperately that the girl would turn around. But she didn't, and the man turned and put his arm around her shoulders, and they walked up out of the shining grass and along the road behind their friends.

Juniper heard more laughter and then the silvery music of the pipes. The cart rumbled on. The scene grew misty again and dark.

Then she saw another light, very high, but still glimmering and indistinct. She thought at first it was a moon or a lantern hung very high; then she realised it was sunlight, glinting in many colours and shaped like arched windows. She smelled flowers and incense. Slowly the darkness lessened, and she could make out huge stone archways rising to a massive vaulted ceiling, the curves and arches forming perfect geometric designs. She lowered her eyes down from the graceful ceiling and the high windows with their luminous glass, down past yawning archways and vast painted pillars, down to the glowing floor and the congregation sitting there. Everything now was light.

The people were all sitting on the floor, and Juniper realised with a shock that she was sitting among them, next to two old women in sombre robes and white veils. She could smell the herbs and sweat in the women's clothes and could hear one of them swallowing all the time as she chewed something.

No one was paying the friar much attention; he was chanting the service in Latin, and his inattentive flock, not understanding, was amusing itself with jokes and chatter, sometimes laughing aloud. Several of the children were dancing around one of the pillars, their arms raised, and they danced as if entwining ribbons around a maypole. Their clothes were bright and colourful in the soft reflected sun.

Juniper smiled to herself and glanced sideways at the old woman next to her.

"By God's blessed bones, 'tis a disgrace," the old woman muttered loudly to her friend. " 'Tis pagan and unchristian. That maypole is an idol, Maud — a cursed idol — and they danced around it all the morn, and now they sit in here as bold as brass, with their flowers and their wanton looks and their cheeks all ruddy from their wicked deeds. And that witch Johanna, she danced more than they all and gave that young man Edmund such looks as charmed away his heart. Bewitched he is — bewitched and hot and so far gone he's thinking he's in Paradise."

"Fie, good Agnes!" cackled the old woman from the other side. "He's allowed to be besotted. They be betrothed. And she's a fair maid, that you must admit."

"I'll admit nothing but that she's a witch!" muttered Agnes. "She scolded the miller not a week gone past, and yesterday he fell down and broke his leg. It was a curse she placed on him. Holy

Jesus save us all from her and all her kind! Take heed — she'll face accusers in the end."

Juniper followed the old woman's gaze and saw the young man Edmund sitting a few rows ahead with the fair-haired girl beside him. Her hair was all disarrayed, the flowers tumbling, the white ribbon hanging half unbound. There were grass stains on the back of her white bodice, and there was a small tear on her left sleeve where the cord sewing it to the dress had broken.

Still Juniper couldn't see her face. She was very tempted to get up and go and sit beside her, but there were other people sitting very close to the girl, all her friends with their flowers and green branches, and there was no room for Juniper. So she sat still and watched the friar in his pulpit, listening to his chant sometimes rising above the hum of voices, sometimes losing itself in the deep, purple echoes; and all the time the sunlight played down upon them from the high windows, the pillars towered upwards into the light, and the vaulted ceiling stretched like wings across the heavens and spanned tomorrow.

A deep peace settled over Juniper; an elation and a sense of belonging. She never lost sight of who she was or where she was from, but her being here seemed right, and in the true order of things. There was no incongruity, no fear. She couldn't help wondering, in an amused way, whether or not she could be seen; and she was almost tempted to lean over and touch Agnes's arm and ask her for the name of the church and the year. But something made her hesitate. An intuition warned her not to disturb a hair or a flower or a fold in a robe, or even the dust on the cool stone floor. She had the feeling that even the smallest disturbance could have stupendous results.

After a while she thought of Dylan, sitting alone in the attic in the light of another time. She closed her eyes and breathed deeply, and gradually the chanting and the voices and the laughter faded, became echoing and dim. The laughter of the children was the last thing she heard. She thought of a door back into her own world and followed the darkness towards it. She took several more deep breaths and opened her eyes.

Colours from her own stained glass window, intensified by the setting sun, poured down across her. She blinked in the light and realised with a surprise that she was crying. Part of her was relieved, greatly relieved, to be back again; but part of her grieved for the place she had left, and she wanted desperately to go back. It was the old homesick feeling again, the unbearable longing and pain, as if the place she had left was her true home, and here she was a stranger.

She wiped her eyes and remembered Dylan.

He was still sitting in front of the drawing, his head bent, his glasses in his hands. He too was crying. She sat beside him and put her arm around his neck and looked at what he had done.

He had drawn the church with the high pillars and the beautiful vaulted ceiling. He had drawn all the people in the congregation — the old women with their dark garments and their veils; the men with their knives at their waists and their wide, folding hats almost like turbans falling down; the children dancing around the pillars, laughing; the friar in his pulpit, calm and unconcerned beyond the people; and he had drawn the girl Johanna, with her long, fair hair and her shoulder touching Edmund's. He had drawn the religious murals on the pillars and on the stone walls behind, the candles and the sunbeams, the baskets of flowers at the people's feet. Some of the people were only quick sketches, but even in those brief lines he had captured the essence of their being: the way a head lifted, listening; the shine of a sword against a velvet cloak; a gnarled, old hand at rest against a folded robe; and the wondering, toothless grin of an old woman. He had drawn Agnes and Maud but not Juniper.

Much of the drawing was unfinished, but what he had done was striking.

He turned his head and looked at her.

"We've flown far and high, you and I," he said.

"I know." She removed her arm from around his neck and wiped her face with her hands. "Did you see the other place as well?" she asked.

He nodded. "I saw it. I saw the road in the dawn, and the people walking and singing, and the oxen and the cart carrying the maypole. But it was too dark to draw, and there was too much movement. I was glad when it changed and I saw the church."

They looked at each other again, tearful and laughing, amazed at where they had been; and Dylan put his hand behind her head, drew her to him, and kissed her.

It was a long time before they moved apart, and then they moved only slightly. They sat with their heads bowed together, their foreheads touching, while there flowed between them a harmony more joyful and strong than anything they had ever known.

"I think I never want to leave this place," said Dylan softly.

"I think I have to," she whispered with a small laugh. "If I don't go to the toilet soon, I'll disgrace myself."

He grinned, and she got up and left the room.

Dylan put his glasses back on and looked again at the drawing he had done. He sighed, tired but happy and supremely satisfied.

It took three days for Dylan to finish the drawing, then four more to paint it. Every day after school he went directly to Juniper's house and worked until one or two in the morning. He didn't stop to eat and often didn't touch the drinks she took him.

While he drew, Juniper sat on the windowseat and did homework or read. She never spoke unless he asked her something; usually it was to discuss a particular colour or a detail on a costume. She offered no comments or advice, nor made any judgements. She watched as the drawing unfolded;

every robe, every braid of hair, every flower and leaf and jewel was drawn with meticulous skill and sensitivity. The drawing was a revelation of another time, accurate in every detail, and utterly beautiful.

Watching it being done, Juniper could hardly believe that the person doing it shared the same plot of earth she did, the same city, the same room. Sometimes he looked up at her, briefly, while he worked, and she knew that he, too, was amazed at what came from his mind and hand. The drawing was a gift, in inspiration and execution above anything else he had ever done.

He finished it on a Sunday afternoon, not long after Juniper came back from having lunch. He had been working since seven that morning, without a break. He put down the paintbrush, took off his glasses, and rubbed his eyes. When he looked up, he saw Juniper watching him. She was lying on her side on the windowseat, propped up on cushions, a book unopened in front of her.

"It's finished," she said.

He nodded, unable to speak. The picture was superb. He could hardly believe it was his.

Juniper knelt beside him and looked at the finished work. He had left only pencilwork around the edges, and in the high, magnificent vaulted ceiling. But below, where the people sat and the friar preached and the children danced, he had gradually brought in the colour, working it more strongly towards the centre, breathing life and light until, in the flowers and flesh and garments of Johanna and her friends, all was fully coloured, alive and radiant.

"It's out of this world," she breathed. "You've excelled yourself, Leonardo."

"So have you," he said. "You've got a fantastic imagination. I almost wish all this was real, and that Johanna and Edmund did exist, somewhere else in time. I suppose there's no way we'll ever find out." He grinned. "Even if I drew her portrait front on, no one we know would recognise her."

"I wish you could draw her face," said Juniper longingly. "I'd love to see her face. Did you see it?"

"No. I only saw what you saw."

"Did you hear the chanting and the talk and the children laughing?"

"Yes. And I smelled the flowers and the incense and herbs . . . and the unwashed clothes."

"Do I detect a slight disapproval of medieval life?"

"None at all. I'd live there tomorrow if I had half a chance. And if you were there."

"I'd be there," she said. "So you want to go on, then? You're not afraid anymore of our weird telepathic talents?"

He smiled, transformed by the sun on his face and by his own ecstasy. "It's flying in Paradise," he said. "I never want it to end."

14

Forebodings

MARSHA looked up quizzically as Juniper came into the kitchen. "He's finished it?" she asked.

Juniper nodded. "He's just cleaning the brushes and putting away the paints."

Marsha turned to the quiche she was making, finished sprinkling the cheese on it, and put it into the oven. When she faced Juniper again, her face was troubled and grave.

"Juniper, are you sure you know what you and Dylan are doing?"

Juniper took a small knife off the bench, selected an apple from the fruit basket, and began peeling it. "Of course we do," she said lightly. "And you promised you'd never ask questions."

"I won't, then," said Marsha. "But I will tell you something. This is affecting Dylan far more deeply than it's affecting you. He's done nothing this week except that picture. His mother called here four times, and he's promised to phone her back — and hasn't. He can't have done any homework, and I know he can't have been in any fit state for school. He wouldn't have slept more than three or four hours a night, all week. I know he's living on creative energy, and I know he's perfectly happy, but he's getting this all out of proportion. It's ruling his life. It's not good, Juniper."

Juniper bit into a piece of apple and wandered out towards the lounge.

"I haven't finished yet!" called Marsha.

Juniper came back into the kitchen, the apple portions in her hands, and leaned nonchalantly against a cupboard. Her face was sulky and defiant. "I haven't twisted his arm, Marsha," she said hotly. "And if you want to know the truth, he hasn't exactly thrilled me all week, either. On Monday I couldn't go to the movies with all my friends because of him. I was going out with Kingsley on Thursday night and had to put him off because Dylan was here. And now he wants to do this image exchange thing again Tuesday, and that's the night of Wendy's barbecue. I know he's getting obsessed about it, but that's not my fault."

Marsha sighed and bit her lower lip. "I thought you'd finished with Kingsley."

"Well, I haven't."

"Does Dylan know that?"

"I told him."

"And what did he say?"

114

"Nothing."

"You know he thinks the world of you, don't you?"

Juniper nodded, and a small, tender smile crossed her face. "I know," she said softly. "He kissed me once. It wasn't horrible, either."

"Are you being fair to him?" asked Marsha.

"I think so. Dylan's just a friend. A good friend — my best and closest and most trusted friend — but Kingsley's my boyfriend."

Marsha looked bewildered. "You've got strange priorities. If you feel closer to Dylan and trust him more than Kingsley, then what's Kingsley doing being the boyfriend?"

Juniper's dark eyes danced, and she grinned and bit into another piece of apple. "He's a great dancer, and he's got a terrific body."

Marsha laughed. "You're incorrigible," she said. "Go and help Dylan clean up the attic. We're going out to Niall's for a picnic dinner by the river. Dylan's invited. But tell him to phone home first. His mother's rung for him twice today."

When Kathy answered the phone she sounded breathless and tense. "Dylan? Oh, thank God. I need you here, now. An hour ago."

"I can't come now, Mum," he said. "We're going out to Niall's for dinner."

"You've been out for dinner every night this week."

"Not to Niall's. Please, Mum. He lives by a river, in a caravan. I'm dying to see it."

"When would you be home?"

"I don't know. Marsha said we wouldn't be late, and she'd drop me off on the way home."

He heard his mother sigh, and for a while she said nothing. Her breathing sounded strange, and he hoped desperately that she wasn't crying.

"I promise I won't be late," he said. "Please, Mum. And I'll stay home tomorrow night. I promise."

"All right. Do what you like," she said in a high, resigned voice. "It doesn't matter, anyway."

She hung up.

For a moment guilt weighed heavily on Dylan, and an urgent feeling swept over him like a warning. Quickly he suppressed it.

"I can go," he said, walking into the lounge. "So long as we're not too late getting back."

Marsha looked at him, an incredulous look on her face. The painting of the medieval abbey was on the table in front of her, and she'd been looking at it while he was on the phone.

"How old are you, Dylan?" she asked.

"Fourteen," he replied, puzzled. "I'll be fifteen in a couple of months. Why?"

Marsha half smiled and looked at him in amazement. "I can't believe it," she murmured. "I can't believe you did this painting."

He blushed. "I suppose that's a compliment," he said. "Thanks. I can hardly believe it myself." He gave Juniper a shy, deep smile. "Anyway, it wasn't only from me," he added.

116

"What did you send him, Juniper?" Marsha asked curiously. "A scene from a film?"

"Something like that," said Juniper, not meeting her mother's eyes.

But Marsha saw the colour deepen in Dylan's face, and though she asked no more questions, she stored the abbey image away in her mind and worried about it.

The river chuckled as it splashed over the rocks, and the summer breeze soughed in the willows. Juniper leaned up on her elbow in the long grass and watched Dylan's quiet face. He was lying on his back in the spangled sunlight, fast asleep. A willow branch hung low over him, and Juniper pulled it down and tickled his face with the leaves. He shook his head and muttered, rolled over, and buried his face in his arms.

"Your scintillating conversation is ruining the peace," she remarked, amused.

"What?" He lifted his head, bewildered and disoriented.

"I said you're talking too much."

He grinned and sat up. "Sorry. You've no idea how tired I am."

"I have, you know. I stayed up with you, remember, all those hours you worked."

"You slept on the windowseat," he said. "You may have been holding an open book, but you slept."

"Tried and found guilty," she said, smiling.

"Why don't you lie down in the caravan on Niall's bed and sleep?"

"It's fine here," he said, lying down again. He looked up at the sun glinting through the green and sighed. "It's like heaven in this place. It must be marvellous living here."

He turned his head and looked through the grass at Niall's caravan parked in a flat place near the river.

It was sheltered by a semicircle of willow trees, facing a gentle stony slope down to the water. In the sunlight its red and yellow paint glimmered and made a burst of colour against the earth. Not far away an old draught-horse grazed, tethered to one of the trees.

"I didn't know it was a real gypsy caravan," said Dylan. "Not a red and yellow one with a little chimney and big wheels and a horse to pull it with."

"What did you think he pulled it with — his motorbike?" she asked, amused.

"No . . . I don't know what I was expecting, really. Something ordinary, I suppose. But that's marvellous. Just like Toad's."

Juniper sat up, startled, "Like *whose*?"

"Toad's. You know. Toad of Toad Hall. He had a gypsy caravan before he discovered the motorcar. Don't you remember?"

Juniper chuckled and relaxed again. "For a moment I thought you had the weirdest friends," she said.

"I do," he smiled. "Would the weirdest of all

like to come for a walk? It'll be cooler down by the river."

"All right — if the weirdest of all is allowed to go and get a drink first. Do you want one? It'll only be water with a squeeze of lemon juice."

"That's fine."

Together they went through the grass over to the caravan and up the bright steps to the cool, dim interior. Niall was inside, sprawled on a wide bed at the back, writing. Behind him was a row of velvet cushions and a curved shelf that ran the full width of the caravan. Books, pottery jars, and bowls of dried lavender brightened the shelf and were lit by a shaft of sunlight from an open window above.

He smiled at them and put down his pen. "Do you want something to eat as well?" he asked, getting up.

"Only a drink," said Juniper, helping herself to two glasses from a small cupboard above the sink and filling them with water from a large pottery jug. "Where's Marsha?"

"Gone for a walk," said Niall. "Why don't you two go for a swim? There's a terrific swimming hole further around. It's my bath, but I'll let you borrow it."

"No thanks," replied Juniper. "Where are your lemons?"

Niall got her one from a string bag hanging in the corner behind her, and Dylan realised that everything in Niall's tiny home had its own place. As he drank his water he looked around, marvelling

119

at the compactness of it all, the careful use made of every precious space, the neatness of every shelf and cupboard. As in a boat, everything was securely fixed; even the windowsills and shelves had wood-turned rails across the front to prevent potted herbs, jars, books, and plates from falling down when the caravan was on the road. Cups hung from hooks in the ceiling; strings of vegetables hung from the sides of hand-carved cupboards; and small, beautiful, original paintings filled spaces between cupboards and above shelves. Everything looked rustic and hand-crafted, from the bright velvet cushions and deep-fringed curtains to the quaint little wood-burning stove.

"You cook on that?" Dylan asked, surprised, looking at the stove. "I saw one of those in a museum once."

Niall laughed. "Mine certainly isn't there for show," he said. "Though mostly I cook over a fire down by the river. It's too hot with the stove on in here this time of year. It's good in the winter, though."

Dylan put his glass down on the small wooden bench and gave Niall a grin. "I bet it's fantastic living here," he said.

"It is."

They heard footsteps on the stairs, and Marsha came in. She was wearing a wide, floppy straw hat and a muslin dress and carried a bunch of wild white daisies. She looked as old-fashioned and charming as the place she came to, and she held out the flowers to Niall.

"I found these for you," she said.

Niall's face softened, and he smiled. He had a beautiful smile, slow and warm and enveloping. "Thank you," he said, taking the flowers.

"Come on," said Juniper, slipping her hand around Dylan's arm. "We'll leave these two in peace and go for a walk." She looked at her watch. "We'll be back in two hours," she added.

She went out down the steps, and Dylan followed her, blushing. She saw his face and laughed.

"Dylan Pidgely, the Innocent," she said, linking her arm in his and sauntering down towards the river. "Don't tell me your father never looks at your mother like that."

"He doesn't actually," said Dylan, trying to ignore the warmth of her thigh against his, as they moved together over the uneven ground. "And she certainly doesn't give him flowers."

"Well, Marsha and Niall have got something special," said Juniper, letting go of his arm and stooping to take off her sandals. She left them on a conspicuous rock and went on to walk in the water's edge. She was wearing a white shirt and white shorts, and looked cool and slender and almost ethereal as she danced from stone to stone in the shining light. Dylan took his sneakers off and left them behind on the rock, too, then caught up with her. He was conscious all over again of her loveliness and warmth, her long brown legs, and the laughing way of her. And he'd believed yesterday that he only loved her mind.

"There's something wrong with today," said

Juniper, slipping on a stone and almost falling. She came back up onto the grass, nearer Dylan, and she seemed pale, less vibrant than before. She looked sideways into his face, and he smiled, his face warm and glowing in the sun, his glasses slightly misted over.

"Don't you feel it?" she asked, stopping.

"Feel what?"

"Something out of tune. Something hanging over us."

He looked up toward the sun, then at her face again. "Only light," he said, bewildered and amused. "There's nothing wrong with today, Juniper. Today's perfect."

"Are you sure?"

"Positive."

She smiled suddenly, relieved, trusting his judgement, and they walked on beyond the riverbend.

The afternoon was perfect in Dylan's eyes. He was very tired, but the wonder of the last week was still with him, and the inspiration and creative energy still carried him high. He basked in the sun and in Juniper's company, totally content.

They discussed art, medieval castles, death, and God; debated the pros and cons of euthanasia, nuclear energy, and nude sunbathing; they argued often, laughing; and they shared long, shining silences.

On the way back to the caravan, while it was still a long way off, they passed again a narrow place in the river where an old tree had died and fallen across the water, making a rough natural bridge.

"Let's go over to the other side," said Dylan impulsively.

"No . . . it's the farmer's land," she said, hesitantly.

"It doesn't make any difference. This is all his land, Niall said. Come on." He was already across the rocks and climbing the dried roots of the tree.

She followed, unsure, afraid.

"What's wrong?" he asked, surprised.

"I . . . I don't like water much," she admitted.

"We're not swimming across," said Dylan, holding out his hand. "We've got a bridge. Here, I'll help you."

Still she hung back.

He laughed, not sure she was serious. "You've crossed five centuries in your mind," he said. "And you won't walk across a simple bridge."

Her eyes sparked, and she pushed out her chin. She followed him up onto the wide trunk, ignoring his offered hand, and balanced behind him on the tree, her arms outstretched, her eyes straight ahead. They came to the branches, and Dylan noticed that the water below was still fairly deep and running swiftly over the rocks. "We'll have to find the main branches and walk on those," he said. He inched along a swinging limb, testing it, and heard a scream and a splash behind him.

Alarmed, he turned and saw Juniper floundering in the river below. The water was only waist deep, but the current was strong and she couldn't gain her balance. Again and again she tried to stand, slipped on the mossy rocks, went underwater, and came up again, gasping and shrieking and waving frantically. Laughing, he waited for her to find her footing. But she didn't, and the current began sweeping her along, under the tree and its broken, jagged branches, and down.

Shocked, he realised that her screams were genuine, and her wild thrashing was not an act. She was beginning to panic. He swung along a branch and dropped into the deeper water, gasping at the icy shock of it, and allowed the force of the river to sweep him along to where she was. She was caught in shallow rapids and was clutching a partly submerged rock, her head above water, weeping and screaming. He slithered over to her, finding his own balance difficult, and bent over her, lifting her.

"It's all right," he called over the tumult of the waters. "It's only thigh deep. Here — hold on to me. We can walk back."

Sobbing and choking, she gripped his arms as he half dragged, half led her towards the bank they had left. The rocks were treacherously slippery, and the rush of the river strong and almost overpowering. Several times they fell and were swept helplessly against the rocks, their limbs tangled and bruising on the stones, the water roaring across their backs. It could have been fun, Dylan thought, if she hadn't been screaming so much. He was almost angry by the time he dragged her up onto the dry stones.

"You didn't half make that difficult!" he panted, sitting beside her on a rock. Looking down, he noticed that one of his knees was deeply cut and bleeding freely. There were grazes and bruises all down his legs, and his ribs ached.

She sat near him, with her knees drawn up and her face buried in her arms. She too was badly grazed along her left arm, and there were mottled bruises along her legs. She was still choking and sobbing and shaking uncontrollably.

He lifted back her heavy, dripping hair and tried to see her face. "Cheer up," he said. "You're all right. You were never in any danger, you know. The water wasn't even up to our waists."

She turned her head away and was quiet. But her breathing was uneven and painful, and her fingers shook.

"Are you hurt?" he asked gently.

She shook her head and glanced at him. The look on her face horrified him. She looked as if she had seen death.

"Are you sure you're not hurt?" he asked in a low voice. "You look awful."

She gave him the ghost of a smile. "Thanks."

He put his arm around her shoulders, and she leaned against him and began to weep quietly.

For a long time he held her, saying nothing, stroking her wet hair back from her face with his white fingers and noticing that his own hands shook.

After a while he noticed that the sun was going down, and they were sitting in the last patch of sunlight on the stones. The wind was cold.

He shivered. "We should go back," he said. "We should get dry and warm." He glanced at his watch. It had been smashed on the rocks and was ruined.

She lifted her head and dried her face on her frozen hands. "I'm sorry," she said hoarsely. "I hate water, Dylan. I've been terrified of it ever since I was a little kid."

"You don't have to apologise," he said, helping her to her feet. "Anyway, it was my fault. You said you didn't want to go across."

They hobbled stiffly along the river shore, aching all over and shivering. As they neared the caravan they smelled wood smoke on the evening wind and saw a fire down by the river. Marsha was beyond it, gathering driftwood.

"You're just in time for dinner," called Niall cheerfully, coming out of the caravan with plates and a salad. He stopped on the bottom step and grinned. "You two went swimming after all?"

"Kind of," muttered Juniper with a wry smile. "Involuntarily. Dylan rescued me."

"What it is to be a hero," murmured Niall, smiling at Dylan. "You know where the towels are, Juniper. Get dried and bring your clothes down to the fire. We'll dry them a bit before you go home."

She looked startled, and he grinned. "There are

two spare blankets in the storage space under the bed. You can wrap up in those."

He went on down to the fire, and Juniper and Dylan went into the caravan. She found the towels and blankets and gave Dylan his. She turned her back on him and started unbuttoning her shirt. "Don't look," she said, over her shoulder.

Obediently he turned away and peeled off his own wet things and folded the rough blanket around him. "Mum would have a fit if she knew I was doing this," he said, shivering.

Juniper laughed and led the way out into the coppery light, her wet clothes in her hand, the blanket like a toga about her. But Dylan felt a great rush of guilt and pain and an unaccountable sense of foreboding. Fighting to ignore it, he went out to the smoky fire and a world aflame with dying light.

15

Hard Times

JUNIPER peered at Dylan over her coffee and smiled. "To my knight in shining sneakers," she said, lifting the cup. Then she pulled the blanket closer around her shoulders and began sipping the drink.

They were sitting together on Niall's bed, still wrapped in their blankets, while their clothes finished drying in front of the hot stove. A thick candle burned on the windowsill behind them, and the caravan was warm and dark. Niall and Marsha were sitting outside on the steps, talking quietly. The sound of their voices drifted in, accompanied by the murmur of the river and the night song of the crickets.

"I feel such an idiot," said Juniper. "I ruined a terrific day."

"No you didn't. If you hadn't fallen in, I

wouldn't be sitting here half naked on Niall's bed, talking to you by candlelight."

She chuckled. "You're hopeless, Dylan Pidgely."

"Hopeful," he corrected.

She looked at him, her face shadowed in the dimness, her eyes secret and deep. "You know you haven't really got a hope, don't you, Dylan?"

"I don't need a hope," he said. "I've got everything I want."

"You're easily satisfied, then."

"I guess so." He shrugged, and the blanket slipped off his shoulder. His skin was flushed in the candlelight, his hair a tawny, shining gold. He had taken his glasses off, and his eyes were a warm, translucent blue.

"You're not really so bad," she said softly. "And you're the only one I'd trust, right here, right now."

He looked at her, one fair eyebrow raised. "Thank you," he said. "But considering we've got two chaperons on the steps out there, I'd say your declaration of trust doesn't hold much water. If you'll pardon the expression."

"It holds more water than you think, Leonardo. Only I'd rather call it sunlight than water."

"Call it sunlight, then," he said. "I like that. A trust full of sun. That amounts to a galaxy's worth."

"It is. And it embraces all time." She leaned over and gave him a soft kiss on the cheek. "And now we'd better get dressed, Dylan Pidgely. We promised your mother you'd be home early. It's

129

already after ten." She hesitated. "You take your clothes outside," she added. "I'll get dressed in here."

"What happened to the trust?" he asked, putting his empty cup on the shelf behind him, pulling the blanket tight, and struggling to the edge of the bed.

"It's gone with the sun," she grinned. "It'll be back in the morning."

"Fraud," he said, as he gathered up his steaming clothes and went outside.

Dylan opened his front door and crept in. He closed the door quietly behind him and locked it. A light was on in the lounge, and his heart sank. She must have waited up. Maybe what she had wanted really was important.

He pushed open the lounge door and peeped in. His father was there, sitting on the sofa, his face buried in his hands.

"Dad?" Dylan went in slowly, aware of something terribly wrong. When his father looked up, Dylan saw that he had been crying.

"Sit down, son," Tom said. "I've got something to tell you."

"Mum?" mouthed Dylan, but no sound came.

"Sit down. This isn't easy. Don't look like that, Dylan. She's not dead. She's all right."

Dylan sat on the edge of a chair, and Tom got up and began pacing the room. Dylan waited, his hands clenched tightly on his thighs, his face white.

Tom stopped in front of the window, looking

out, his back to his son. The curtains hadn't been drawn, and the dark glass was covered with frantic moths.

"She's gone," said Tom, so quietly that Dylan could hardly hear. "She's gone. Left us. She went this afternoon sometime." His voice broke, and he passed his hands across his face. He waited a while, then spoke again. "The twins were here by themselves when I got home. They'd been cooking. They could have burnt the house down."

Dylan stood up and went into his parents' bedroom. All her things were gone from the dressing table. He pulled open the wardrobe door. Her side was empty. Even her shoes were gone.

He went back into the lounge and sat down again. "Why?" he asked.

"I suppose you have a right to know," said Tom, still with his back to him. "The twins think she's gone for a holiday. I'll explain more to them tomorrow. But you may as well know the truth. I was seeing someone else."

"Having an affair?"

"I'd rather not call it that."

"Who with?" Dylan's voice was high with astonishment.

"With Evelyn Honeyburn."

"The birdcage woman?"

"For God's sake, Dylan, do you have to make it sound so ordinary?"

"Sorry."

"It wasn't anything shallow, Dylan. And I never

meant it to happen. But it did, and I had more happiness with her in one afternoon than I've had with your mother in the last twenty years."

Dylan thought of Marsha and Niall, of the tender smiles and the warmth and the gentleness, and suddenly saw his father in a new light.

"Wow, Dad," he breathed. He was smiling without realising it.

Tom turned around, surprised, and saw the look on his son's face. He sat down, stunned, and ran his hands over his bald patch, smiling himself.

Then Dylan's face became grave and desolate. "It's tough for Mum, though," he said.

Tom sighed. "Well, she certainly didn't applaud me."

"How did she find out?"

"She asked, so I told her."

"This afternoon?"

"Last night. I was working this afternoon. At a timber yard. That's another thing. I've got a job. It means big changes for all of us. I'm afraid you'll have more responsibility here, now. With your mum gone and me working, you'll have to do a lot of the housework and get dinner every night. I'm sorry, but that's how it is. Later on, when I can think straight, I might get someone in to help. But for now we've all got to pull together. I'm sorry. You won't be able to go around to Juniper's any-more. My job includes weekend work if I want it, and right now we need the extra money. The twins are too young to leave by themselves. You'll have to be here, Dylan, every day. I don't ever want to come home again and find them by themselves. You understand?"

Dylan nodded.

"Good. I need you now, son. We all need each other. We'll get through this somehow, and maybe in time your mum will come back. But right now all we have is each other. I won't be seeing Evelyn again. I give you my word on that. I don't expect you to make sacrifices and not make them myself. Does all this seem fair to you?"

Again Dylan nodded. He couldn't speak.

Tom got up and put a hand on Dylan's bent shoulder. "Go to bed now, Dylan. It's time you had a good night's sleep. If you can. Are your clothes damp?"

"Yes. We fell in the river." It seemed a million years ago.

Dylan got to his feet and somehow found himself hugging his father. Then he pulled away quickly and fled to his room.

He stripped off his damp clothes and got into his pyjamas. His bed wasn't made. He straightened it out, then went over to his desk and took the portrait of Juniper out from between the pages of a book.

Only then he wept.

16

The Silver Chalice

HE next eight weeks were a nightmare for Dylan. If he could have talked freely with Juniper at school, it wouldn't have been so bad; but there he was only on the outer edge of her circle of friends. She sat with him sometimes in their lunch hours, but always her other friends interrupted to whisk her away for a game of tennis or a walk, and he didn't accept her invitations to join them. He suspected that her friends thought her friendship with him was a joke. He was still very much the outsider, unliked and alone.

Most of Juniper's lunch hours were spent with Kingsley, and when she was with him Dylan buried himself in a book and didn't emerge until the bell went. It hurt Dylan that even now she didn't place her time with him above her time with anyone else.

Her remoteness at school had always hurt him, but now, when they had nothing else, it grieved him deeply. Still, he said nothing, grateful for her friendship on any terms.

Only on the phone was there the old easiness between them, and her calls were the only sane and beautiful thing in his life. Often she rang late at night, just as he'd finished ironing the twins' clothes for tomorrow, or put away his homework, or finished a late coffee with his father. She always seemed to know exactly when to ring, and her calls were always warm, amusing, inspiring, and immensely encouraging. She could make him laugh at even the most horrific things the twins did, and many times she lifted him up out of depression and despair. An hour on the phone with her could wipe out a week's misery.

But still he hungered for the deeper communion; the glory and the mystery of her visions, and the incredible power and oneness of sharing them. He missed the light, the flying, the joy — missed them with a hunger and a longing that bordered on physical pain. He realised now the full extent of their telepathic oneness, and how deeply it had bound them. With Juniper, with even just the sound of her voice, all the world spun true and jubilant. But without her, and without the unity with her visions and her joy, all was deathly grey, off-centre, and without meaning.

So he battled his way through the days, fighting to keep the twins under control, struggling to keep up with washing, ironing, shopping, housework, and meals; being given detentions constantly for homework not done or for falling asleep in class; and often being late for school because one of the twins had lost her schoolbag or her shoes or was just having another howling session for her mother.

Tom did his best to help, but he left for work at seven-thirty in the mornings and didn't get home until twelve hours later. He often worked weekends as well. He, too, was grappling with grief, weariness, and not a small amount of temptation; and though he was aware of his son's trials, he could do little to alleviate them.

So life in the Pidgely home went on, often noisy and painful and sometimes desperate; and all the peace-keeping and organisation fell on Dylan. Then one night he had a phone call from Juniper that was like a reprieve from prison.

"Dylan? Can you talk now?"

"Yes. The twins are just getting into bed. How are you?"

"Fine. Terrific. Marvellous. Are you busy after school tomorrow? I mean — are you desperately, positively busy, or can you spare an hour?"

"I can spare the rest of my life," he said. "I'm going to go mad tonight, and in the morning they're going to cart me off to a rest-home. I won't ever have to find another sock or sew another eye on a teddybear or iron another dress. And just in case that doesn't happen, the twins are going to a birthday party after school tomorrow, and I don't have to have anything to do with them until six o'clock.

136

I have two hours. Two whole hours. Where do you want to go — Paradise?"

"I'm halfway there already," she said. "Something marvellous happened today. You know that old professor friend I told you about? Vincent Gilroy?"

"Has he died?"

"Don't be awful. He's going to England next month to live. He said he doesn't want to take everything with him, and he's got something for me."

"The medieval goblet," said Dylan, smiling.

"Yes. I'm going to see him tomorrow to get it. Would you like to come? I'd love you to meet him. And you could show him your drawing of Johanna and everyone in church."

"Would he be interested?"

"Interested? Dylan, he'd be rapt! He loves churches and art. He's got an original drawing by Picasso."

"That's hardly the same as a Pidgely, is it?"

"The first two letters are the same. And the talent's about equal, I'd say."

"You exaggerate beautifully. Is the chalice going to be yours for always, or is he just lending it to you while he's away?"

"Tomorrow it's mine for ever. And if I die, you can have it. It's not to go to a museum. I want us to have a special shared drink out of it, like a ceremony. Marsha's donated one of her best bottles of red wine, and I've turned it into hippocras."

"What's that? Some kind of frog?"

"Careful, Leonardo. It's spiced wine. I used a genuine medieval recipe, with all the right herbs and spices. Marsha thinks I've ruined it. It smells like cough mixture."

Dylan chuckled. "Then you probably have ruined it," he said.

"No I haven't. I know what I'm doing."

"Not fully. At the moment you're holding me up from reading the twins a story. Can I phone you back later?"

"No, sorry. I'm going out with Kingsley."

"Have fun."

"Probably not. He's got a cold-sore on his lip and I can't kiss him."

"I thought you believed in living dangerously."

"Not that dangerously. Travelling to the fifteenth century, maybe, and risking death in the Hundred Years' War; but not kissing Kingsley with a cold-sore. Be real, Dylan."

"My apologies. Go out and have an awful time, then, and I'll see you tomorrow."

"Thanks. I will. 'Bye."

Vincent Gilroy spread Dylan's drawing out on the polished oak table and looked at it for a long time without speaking. Then he looked across at Dylan, his bushy eyebrows raised, his piercing blue eyes intent and admiring.

"You're a very talented young man," he said. "Not only is your artwork magnificent, you've also done your research. Every detail is correct."

Dylan glanced at Juniper quickly, then back at the professor again. The colour rose in his face. "Actually . . . Juniper helped with the details," he muttered.

The blue eyes narrowed, and the old man gave him a slow, questioning smile. "Juniper doesn't know all this, Dylan — not the heraldic designs on the leather knife sheaths, and the way the women did their hair, or the headgear the men wore. You've studied medieval art and costume very closely. This is a credit to you."

Vincent bent over the drawing again, marvelling at it. He had a fine old face, deeply lined, but still lively and handsome beneath a mass of smooth white hair, and a soft, widely curling moustache. His clothes, like his house, were formal, tidy, and incredibly old-fashioned. He leaned forward and pointed to the ceiling of the church in the drawing.

"That's particularly well drawn," he observed. "That nave was built in 1330, you know. Outstanding, isn't it? Tewkesbury Abbey, one of my favourites. It's not as elaborate as some of the bigger churches, but I prefer its simplicity. You've drawn it very well."

"You know which one it is?" croaked Dylan, astounded.

Juniper moved slightly, her eyes wide and intense. She hadn't told Vincent about the way the drawings were done. She had told him only that Dylan drew medieval things.

"Of course I recognise it," said Vincent. "I've been in that nave many times. It's full of chairs now, of course, and the paintings of the Bible scenes have worn off the walls and the pillars. But you've drawn it exactly as it would have been in the fifteenth century. This shows amazing insight into medieval life. It's remarkable, truly remarkable. I cannot tell you how impressed I am and how glad I am to meet you. Would you mind sending me a photograph of this sometime? I'd be extremely grateful. You really are an extraordinary young man."

Dylan nodded, overwhelmed.

But Juniper was gripping the edge of the table, her face white.

"She's real!" she murmured, stunned, lost somewhere between gladness and terror.

"Who's real?" asked Vincent.

"Johanna," said Dylan faintly, half smiling. "The girl with the long fair hair, who's going to marry Edmund. She really was a living person. She lived in Tewkesbury, in the fourteen hundreds."

"Who's Edmund?" asked Vincent, perplexed. "Someone you read about?"

But Juniper and Dylan were suddenly embracing one another, laughing, crowing like triumphant two-year-olds. "She's real!" cried Juniper, on the verge of tears. "I haven't just imagined it all! Oh, Dylan, she's real!"

Vincent scratched his head. "I'm very pleased about that, if you are," he said. "But who is she?"

Juniper disentangled herself from Dylan's arms, and they both sat down opposite Vincent. Breathlessly, her words tumbling, Juniper told Vincent all about the drawings and how they were done.

"Are you telling me you experience time outside your own?" he asked when she had finished, his voice quavering.

Juniper's smile was radiant. "It's marvellous, Vincent. It's like flying. It's the most amazing, brilliant feeling."

Vincent got up and poured himself a straight whiskey. He downed it in two gulps, then poured himself another. This time he put water in it. "Would you two like a drink?" he asked.

Dylan nodded, but Juniper shook her head. "No thanks, we're biking home," she said. "Dylan's lethal enough on a bike as he is. Do you know anything about time travelling, Vincent?"

Vincent sat down and swirled the fiery liquid in his glass. "I'd have thought it was a lot more lethal than riding a bike," he said.

Juniper laughed. "Believe me, he's safer sitting in the attic, time travelling. We're both perfectly safe, Vincent. It's done through meditation, that's all."

"And that's perfectly safe, is it?" murmured Vincent, eyeing them both intently. "You make it sound so casual, Juniper. It's not. It's a very special gift. You are both extremely privileged."

"Have you ever done anything like it?" asked Dylan.

"Not consciously," replied the old man, sipping his whiskey. "But I had a dream once. It was fifty years ago, not long after I bought the silver chalice.

I dreamed I saw a young girl. She had long fair hair, and she carried a white dove. She was obviously from medieval times. But it wasn't just her physical appearance that made the dream memorable. It was her personality, her strength. The dream affected me deeply. I've never forgotten it."

Slowly, Juniper smiled. "I've seen the same girl, Vincent," she said, in a low voice. "The first time was when I was small, soon after the first time you showed me the chalice."

"And you've seen her since?" asked Vincent.

"Yes. Once outside the doorway of a half-timbered house. We didn't bring that drawing. In that, too, you can't properly see her face. And we think this may be her, sitting in the abbey with the man in the blue coat. I heard one of the old women call her Johanna. She also called her a witch. Johanna yelled at the miller, apparently, and a few days later he fell over and broke his leg."

"That was pretty damning evidence," said Vincent, gravely, looking at the grass-stained white bodice and the long bound golden hair. "She walks on a razor's edge." He looked at Juniper again, his blue eyes deep and disturbing. "Take care, my friend. There's a strong connection between you and her. You're similar souls, I think."

Juniper smiled, but her face was tense. "*Is* what Dylan and I do dangerous?" she asked.

"Only in that the slightest disturbance could alter human history," he replied. "I'd say it's perfectly safe to observe the people. But don't touch anything. And no matter what happens, don't try to alter it."

"I knew that," said Juniper, looking at the drawing. "When I was sitting there with Agnes in church, I wanted to talk to her, but something stopped me. I had the feeling that even a word could have far-reaching results. Like a tiny stone dropped into a pool and making vast ripples. So I said nothing."

Vincent nodded, relieved, and finished his whiskey. "I don't know why I worry about you, Juniper," he grinned. "You're an old soul, and wise. Follow your own intuitions. They're your truest guide." He turned to Dylan. "And what about you, young man? How do you feel about this exceptional gift of yours?"

Dylan smiled and blushed. "I love it," he said. "While I'm drawing what Juniper sends, I feel in tune with the whole universe."

"Maybe you are," murmured Vincent. "Carl Jung believed in a power he called the collective unconscious — a huge network of knowledge outside time and space, which can somehow be hooked into by individuals, connecting them with the wisdom of other souls. It explains how races with no earthly connection and totally different cultures can have identical myths; and how two people on opposite sides of the world can be inspired to write exactly the same story. And it explains how some of us know things we have never been taught. Maybe somewhere in that vast pool of knowledge there's something of Johanna, and that's what you two touch. Or maybe you do actually move through what we call time. And speaking of time . . . didn't you say you have to be home by six?"

Dylan looked at the grandfather clock against one wall. "Yes, I do," he said. "I've got to be home before the twins. Otherwise they'll take off somewhere and I'll never find them."

"You'd lose them? With your telepathic abilities?" said Vincent with a faint smile. "I doubt it, Dylan. I doubt it."

He shuffled out, and Dylan shot Juniper a broad grin. "I never thought of that," he said. "These telepathic powers could come in handy for all sorts of things."

"I tried to tell you that," she said, amused. "I told you this could change your life."

"It already has," he said.

Vincent came back, carrying something wrapped in a dark blue velvet cloth. He handed it to Juniper, who unwrapped it carefully and held it out towards Dylan.

"Hold it," she said, smiling. "You won't break it."

He took it in his hands, awed.

It was a heavy chalice, solid silver, with intricate geometric designs engraved around the rim and halfway down. It was inlaid with amethysts, and they glowed a deep, vivid purple. He lifted it towards the light, admiring it, loving its beauty, its solid weightiness, and its great age. For a moment he thought he smelled strange, sweet herbs, and felt a high, lilting joyfulness, like a song.

"It is Johanna's chalice," he said with a smile, knowing it with everything in him. And he handed it to Juniper as if it were the most precious thing he had ever touched.

17

My Sister, My Self

OM peered around the twins' bedroom door and saw the girls sitting up on Barbara's bed, one on either side of Dylan, and he was reading to them. It was his well-worn, beloved *The Wind in the Willows*, and he was reading the powerful, shining part where Rat and Mole, looking for the lost baby otter, find him at the feet of the Piper at the Gates of Dawn. Robyn was spellbound, as breathless and awed as Rat and Mole had been; but Barbara was dozing, her arms around her teddybear.

Tom smiled to himself and went out, closing the door quietly.

Dylan finished the chapter, closed the book, and slid it carefully under Barbara's pillow. Robyn lifted her curly head from his shoulder and asked seriously: "Will that Friend and Helper be looking after Mummy, too, and playing her that music?"

Dylan thought for a long time. "Mum's not lost, like little Portly was," he replied at last. "She's looking after herself."

"Only lost children get looked after?"

"It's a story, Robyn. Things happen in stories that don't always happen in real life."

"But it's true, isn't it? Rat and Mole and Toad and the Piper — they're all real."

"I don't know, Robyn. Maybe they are, somewhere. I hope so."

"Mummy said stories aren't true. She says they're made up. She says fairies aren't real, either. But I know they are. I've seen one."

"You're very lucky, then," said Dylan.

Robyn jumped up and went over to her own bed and burrowed in. Dylan cleared the books and toys carefully off Barbara's bed and tucked her in. She murmured in her sleep but didn't wake. Then he went over to Robyn's bed and leaned over her, straightening the blankets. She wound her arms around his neck, and he hugged her and kissed her cheek. Then he turned out their light and went out into the kitchen.

Tom had already finished the dishes, and he'd cut the lunches for the next day.

"Thanks, Dad," said Dylan. "Sorry I didn't help. We read for a bit longer tonight."

"It was the quietest they've been for weeks," grinned Tom. "It'd have been a crime to disturb them. Do you want coffee?"

"Later," replied Dylan. "I've got a stack of homework. I'd better get on with it."

It was eleven before they sat down together for the coffee.

"Nice to see you looking a bit happier," remarked Tom, handing Dylan his drink and sitting on the sofa beside him. "Had a good time with Juniper, did you?"

"Yes. We went to see a friend of hers. Vincent Gilroy. He used to teach medieval history at university."

"And what made her think you'd want to meet him?"

"I like medieval things, too."

"Do you? I never realised that. Is that what you're reading about all the time? History?"

"Some of the time. I read a lot of fiction as well."

"And Juniper's into history, too? Don't tell me that's what you two talk about."

Dylan smiled and sipped his coffee, and said nothing.

"You're a dark horse, you are," said Tom, amused. "You and Juniper must have something special for her to stick with you through all this. The other boyfriend's been given the boot, has he?"

"No. He's still her boyfriend."

Tom grinned. "Sounds about as complicated as my love life."

"Can't be. How are things with you, Dad? I mean . . . do you . . . you must miss Evelyn."

"Yes, I do. And I don't mind admitting I've been badly tempted to go and see her sometimes. But I promised your mother I wouldn't, and I promised you. I still want Kathy back, you know."

"I admire you for that, Dad. Not going back, I mean. And being faithful to Mum, even though she's not here."

"I just hope it's not too late," sighed Tom. "Your mum's not one to compromise. It's all or nothing. That's why she's had so much trouble dieting. It couldn't be just one biscuit; it had to be the whole packet. That's why she gave up the piano, too. She couldn't make a proper career out of it, so she gave it up altogether. Sold her piano, everything. It's the first thing I'll buy her when she comes back."

Dylan was astounded. "A piano? Mum plays the piano?"

"Yes. Didn't you know?"

"No. What sort of career? Teaching the piano?"

"Playing at concerts, Dylan. She was well on the way to becoming a concert pianist. When I met her, she had just won a scholarship to study for three years in Paris. She didn't go because of me. We got married and had you kids. And we'd invested a lot of money in a company that went bust. That's how we ended up in this mess. It was just before she got pregnant with you. And then she had the twins, and that was definitely the end of any career. By then we couldn't even afford a

149

piano, let alone overseas trips. And she's always believed that when you have kids, your first responsibility's to them."

"How come she left, then?"

"I guess she suddenly realised that she's a person, too. I don't know; maybe she'll take up music again. She's had a lot of disappointment and pain in her life, Dylan. I reckon my seeing Evelyn was the last straw. Maybe she suddenly thought all the sacrifice wasn't worth it."

"I've lived with her all my life," said Dylan in a low voice, "and I never knew the most important things about her."

"And I lost sight of them," said Tom. "An awful lot can go on inside a person, and they never show it. I guess the main thing is to talk." He grinned. "And you and Juniper sure do enough of that. You were two hours on the phone the other night."

"If it bothered you, you should have said."

"Didn't bother me. Might have bothered someone trying to ring us, though."

"No one else ever does. Only Juniper."

"You'll have to bring her around here sometime, Dylan. You spent enough time at her place. Why don't you ask her to dinner one night?"

"She wouldn't like my cooking."

"I'll cook, then."

"I wouldn't risk it. Last time you cooked, we got green eggs."

"It was only food colouring. I did it for a joke."

"Forget it, Dad. Anyway, she's usually with Kingsley."

"Please yourself. By the way, I'm not working this weekend. You can have the whole two days off."

Dylan's face broke into a smile. "Thanks, Dad."

Tom dug in his back pocket and took out his wallet. He gave Dylan a twenty-dollar bill. "And take that girl to the movies, or do something exciting for a change, instead of discussing mouldy old history."

Dylan's smile widened, and he pocketed the money. "Thanks. I'm sure we'll think of something."

The attic was balmy and glowing and as beautiful as Dylan remembered it. Juniper had put out some paper already, and it shone in the bright midday sun, the pencils gleaming beside it.

Juniper placed the chalice in a pool of light on the floor beside the paper and smiled at Dylan. "Maybe that'll make the connection stronger," she said.

"How much stronger do you want it?" he asked. "Medieval cooking smells as well, and unwashed clothes, and the stink of raw street sewage?"

"That'd be nice," she said. "Seriously, Dylan, I want to see her face this time. I want to know exactly what she looks like. You'll draw her well, won't you? Every detail?"

He sat cross-legged in front of the paper and picked up a pencil. "I'll draw well whatever you send me," he said.

She sat on the windowseat, and for a long time said nothing. Dylan glanced at her, enquiringly, and noticed that her eyes were closed as if she were already meditating.

"Aren't you going somewhere else?" he asked.

Her eyelids flickered open. "There's no need to anymore," she said. "We can be in the same room, it doesn't matter. Would that bother you?"

"I think I could suffer it." He smiled and closed his eyes.

After a few minutes he opened them. Juniper was lying on her back on the windowseat, her eyes closed, her hands peaceful at her sides. She was wearing her white cotton dress again, and the sun lay in a golden sheen on her legs and arms and face, and glimmered redly in her hair. Her face was tranquil and very still.

"Close your eyes, Leonardo," she murmured, without opening her own. "Keep your mind on the job, or I will have to go."

He swallowed nervously and did as he was told.

The peace of this place was breathtaking. Being here again was like coming home; it was like the sun after a storm, or freedom after a long, terrible internment. Here the world spun true again, and every part of his being rejoiced. He floated in the peace; alert, serene, and completely passive. Slowly, the image came.

It was like a faint light at first; a glimmering in

the darkness, indistinct and dreamlike. Then it became a candle flame, and then a lamp, and finally a shaft of sunlight.

It came from a window, heavily surrounded by wooden beams, but with the shutters opened wide. A wooden trestle-table was beneath the window, scattered with roots and leaves of wild herbs. Two small glass bowls sat on the windowsill, and the sun glinted in the crimson wine they contained and on the deep purple berries soaking there. Everything was touched with a special radiance; an aura that lay on everything, flooding it with unearthly shine.

A hand reached down to the table and placed a silver chalice there. One finger was encircled with a gold ring bearing a small purple stone. The chalice was engraved and set with amethysts.

Juniper's breath caught in her throat. Slowly she lifted her gaze and moved it along the hand and arm, up over the shoulder, to the woman's face.

It was Johanna — Johanna laughing with a child in her arms and with red wine still on her lips. But even now Juniper could not see all her face. She saw it only in profile; saw that her eye was slanted upwards and was brilliant blue in the sunlight. She saw that Johanna's skin was bronzed from her long sojourns in the fields to gather plants; that her hair was long, smooth, and beautifully braided, and fell almost to her knees; and that she was very young — no older than Juniper herself. She saw how tenderly she held her child, and how deeply she loved him. She saw how he tugged at his mother's hair, and how she took his small hands in one of her own and held them still. Then she saw Johanna look up, surprised, her laughter fading, her face intent and alert, as if she listened.

Then, to Juniper's joy and amazement, Johanna turned and faced fully in her direction. She saw the blue eyes look through her and beyond her and come back again. Slowly, incredibly, they focused on Juniper's face.

For a moment they looked at each other, stunned and enthralled. Then Johanna made the sign of the cross on her breast and folded her arms more tightly about her child. But there was, in that shining moment, more wonder and delight than either of them had ever known. And they smiled at each other; and then Juniper moved back again into the darkness and the place where her own world was, and the last thing she saw was the soft gleam of Johanna's hair and the glimmer of her hand as she lifted it again in the sign of the cross.

Slowly, unwillingly, Juniper began to breathe deeply, and to be aware of her limbs heavy on the windowseat and of the sun burning her through the glass. She opened her eyes and for a while lay looking at the attic ceiling. She could hear the soft movements of Dylan's hand and pencil on the paper; heard him sigh and put the pencil down. Gradually, she sat up and looked at what he had done.

He glanced up and turned the drawing so she could see it, his eyes on her face. She gave a low cry and covered her face with her hands.

"What is it?" he asked, getting up and limping over to her. His legs had pins and needles, and he was so thirsty he could hardly speak. He sat close beside her and looked down at the drawing. "What's wrong with it, Juniper?"

"Nothing," she said, dropping her hands. "Nothing. It's perfect. It's Johanna, exactly as she was when she saw me. Half smiling, and as amazed and terrified as I was. It's beautiful, Dylan."

She started to cry, quietly, but with great tearing sobs that came from deep within. Alarmed, not knowing what it was that moved her, Dylan put his arm around her shoulder and offered her his handkerchief. She sobbed a long time, saying half-coherent, anguished, happy things he didn't understand.

"She's like me," she wept, finally, lifting her head from Dylan's shoulder and blowing her nose. "I've never felt like that with anyone in my whole life. It was as if we recognised one another, Dylan. As if she were my sister. Or my self."

"Vincent said the connection was strong between you," Dylan said gently. "He said you had similar souls. Maybe that's what it is: a strong spiritual connection. Maybe your soul touched hers even before you were born. And maybe that's why you've always loved medieval things, always loved cathedrals and doves and dried flowers and ancient music, and light. She loved all those things as well. Did you notice the little clay dove on the leather thong around her neck?"

Juniper wiped her eyes again and looked more

closely at the drawing. There was an open door across the stone floor behind Johanna, and bunches of herbs, vegetables, and berries covered the wall beside it. There was a rocking cradle behind her, too, with flowers and doves carved into the wood.

Johanna's face was lovely, haunting and elfin and other-worldly. It was only in pencil and unfinished, yet Dylan had somehow made her eyes shine, and the sun from the window drenched her skin and clothes and bathed her in a holy light. Her child glanced over his shoulder, looking at the same place she looked, and both pairs of eyes were radiant and surprised.

"Their eyes watch us," said Juniper. "And yet they're not unsettling. Just haunting and beautiful. I don't know how you do it."

He looked at his hands, linked lightly together across his thighs, and he smiled. "I don't know, either," he said. "It's as if they're not really mine, these drawings I do here. They're gifts. I'm just the hands they come through, that's all."

Juniper took his nearest hand and lifted it to her lips and kissed it. "You're an amazing artist, Leonardo," she said. "You'll be famous one day, and all the kids at school now are going to marvel then, because they had the honour to sit with you and know you and walk the same ground, and they never realised it."

"You do," he said, "and you're the only one who matters." He hesitated, then asked: "Do you think we'll be friends all our lives?"

" 'I doubt it not;' " she replied, smiling, " 'and all these woes shall serve for sweet discourses in our times to come.' "

"What are you talking about? There aren't any woes."

"Shakespeare again. Romeo to Juliet when she asked him if he thought they'd ever meet again. They were parting for the last time."

"Are you trying to drop subtle hints?"

Juniper glanced at her watch and gasped. "I wasn't, but I should. It's five-thirty! Kingsley's coming soon, for dinner. Sorry."

"Sorry he's coming or sorry I'm going?"

"Both. I wanted us to have that hippocras from the chalice. That'll have to wait. Do you realise that those few seconds with Johanna were five hours in our time?"

"Yes. If you let go my hand, I'll leave."

She released him, and he stood up, reluctantly. He was going to put the drawing away, but she told him to leave it. "You can come back tomorrow and work on it again," she said, as they went downstairs. "Unless you've got something else you'd rather do."

"Nothing else in all the world," he said. "Enjoy the party tonight."

"I'll try to." She watched as he got on his bike, and as he was about to go she asked, curiously: "Do you ever have the feeling, while you're going down the road, that the cars and bikes and trucks are all unfamiliar and incredible? As if you've always only walked on dusty tracks, and these sealed roads and vehicles and traffic lights are somehow alien and marvellous?"

"No. I don't have time to wonder about things like that. Last time I daydreamed on the road, I hit a dog."

"Go home," she said. "I'll see you in the morning."

He biked off, and she went back up the steps and into the house. Marsha was still out taking her aerobics class, so Juniper went into the kitchen and started preparing dinner. Suddenly she put down the lettuce and leaned heavily against the bench, her hands curled into tight fists. She felt the room spin; felt out of tune and greatly disturbed, as if an inner voice shrieked a warning across her mind. But the words, though loud and disconcerting, were unclear.

She dried her hands and went out to the lounge to put on some music. She turned the stereo up loud and went back to the kitchen. But all evening she felt restless and apprehensive. She didn't want to go out with Kingsley but had no reasonable excuse not to. She went, uneasily, and laughed and danced and was witty and talkative as usual.

But by midnight she could no longer pretend. By midnight, her inner voice was thunderous and terrifying.

18

Ordeal by Water

HE music was loud and vibrant, the lounge crowded. Everyone was dancing, forced into closeness by the crowd, and Kingsley danced with his arms around Juniper, his face against her hair. She was quiet now, almost remote, and there was no bounce in her step.

"What's wrong?" he asked loudly in her ear. "Do you want another drink?"

She shook her head and looked up. "No thanks. Actually, I'd like to go home."

"What? I didn't hear."

"Can we go outside and talk?"

"I thought you'd never ask." He grinned and took her hand, and they fought their way through the dancers out onto the terrace. Here the music still sounded loud, but they could hear themselves talk. Several of their friends were out here too, enjoying the cool air and smoking.

"I want to go home," said Juniper, and Kingsley leaned over to a white wooden table and picked up another can of beer. He tore the tab off and took a long drink.

"Why?" he asked. "Aren't you enjoying yourself?"

"I was. But I want to go." She felt like screaming at him. "I told you an hour ago that I wanted to leave."

"And I said yes, when I'm ready. I'm the driver, remember? We go when I want to go. Besides, it's an hour's drive. I didn't come all this way just to stay for a couple of hours."

"I want to go, Kingsley."

He sipped his beer, his blue eyes narrowed and angry. He was extremely good-looking, but his angled jaw and chin had a hardness about them and an obstinacy that she knew well.

"I'll get a taxi home, then," she said, brushing past him and going back into the house. Eventually she found the phone and started dialling.

A hand tore the receiver out of hers and slammed it down again. "No one," hissed Kingsley, in her ear, "but no one walks out on me. I'll take you home, but you can wait until I've finished my beer."

"I'll go and wait in the car, then," she said.

She walked off, and he watched her go, his eyes bitter, his mouth twisted and grim. Then he swore and followed her out. He unlocked the car and they got in, both furious, neither saying a word.

He sat in the car and finished his beer, slowly, staring ahead down the dark street.

Juniper covered her face with her hands and fought to remain calm. She was overwhelmed by the feeling that she should get out and walk. Yet she sat there, feeling trapped, threatened, and terrified.

"I don't know what's wrong with you," said Kingsley harshly, winding the car window down and throwing the can out. He started up the car, rammed it into gear, and pulled out from the kerb, wheels squealing. "I've had enough of your moods and your excuses, Juniper Golding. You might be able to twist that nerd Pidgely around your little finger, but you're not twisting me. I bet you walk all over him, and he doesn't even whimper. He probably thinks he's honoured. Well, I don't. I've had enough. I'm sick and tired of fitting in with what you want."

The car careered around a corner, narrowly missing a parked truck, and Juniper screamed at him to slow down. He ignored her. They were leaving the suburb now, heading out into the country. He put his foot down on the accelerator, and the speedometer swung up higher and higher. The wind from his open window whipped through the car, and he wound the window up.

"You don't even know what you want, do you?" he went on, savagely. "All week you fob me off with great promises for Saturday night, and when Saturday comes you want to go home early. I can't make you out anymore. I never know what you want, from one hour to the next. I bet you don't know yourself. Well, I know what I want, Juniper. I want a girl who's considerate and predictable, who'll go along with what *I* want for a change and fit in with *my* plans and want to be with *me* rather than her other friends. I'm not being second choice. I'm not being used. I've enjoyed being with you, most of the time, when we've been together — when you haven't been stuck up in the attic with Pidgely. I honestly can't think what you do with him. But whatever it is, I bet he's a pushover."

"You don't know what you're talking about!" she cried angrily. "So shut up and slow down."

"I bet you're doing one of your sick psychic things with him," he went on. "You'll twist the poor bastard's brain, ruin him for life."

"Shut up!"

The car squealed around a bend, close to a bank, and Juniper covered her face with her hands.

"Don't tell me you actually like the little creep," said Kingsley, laughing, glancing at her. "Do you?"

"Watch where you're going!" she yelled, taking down her hands. "And for God's sake, slow down!"

She stared out at the night rushing past, all her nerves jangling. "What's between Dylan and me is none of your business," she added. "You don't own me."

"Thank God for that! I'd have to keep you on a ball and chain to know where you were."

"I pity the person you marry," she said fervently. "You're the biggest chauvinist pig I've ever met. Your attitude to women is medieval."

"Well, you should know all about that, my lady. You're the one who lives with straw on the floor, not me."

"Sometimes I hate you, Kingsley Blayd."

"So why are you with me now?"

She didn't answer but watched the grey road streak away beneath them, and the banks and trees of the narrow gorge loom and vanish in the cold car lights.

"Why are you here, then?" he asked, again. "Better still, tell me what the nerd's got that I haven't. Maybe I could learn something."

They tore around a sharp bend, tyres spinning on the metal edge, and Juniper was flung hard against her door. Her seatbelt bit across her ribs, and she cried out: "Slow down! You'll kill us!"

"For once, I'm calling the tune!" he shouted. "Tell me about Pidgely and what you two do all the time. Go on, tell me!"

She turned away from him, distraught, and looked out her window. She could see the thin white wooden rail that edged the road along the gorge, and beyond it the wild, black, rushing river. All her terrors and uncertainties rushed into one vast, tumultuous fear.

"I'm waiting," said Kingsley harshly, pulling hard on the wheel as the car screamed around another bend. "What's he got that I haven't?"

"Humility," she replied in a low voice.

"Okay," said Kingsley with a tense smile. "I can go along with that. What else?"

"Gentleness." Her voice was so low, he could hardly hear it above the roar of the engine.

"Speak up," he said impatiently. "Did you say gentleness? He could hardly have anything else, could he? He's probably got a rubber backbone."

"Gentleness," she repeated. "And strength enough to let me be myself."

"Interesting. Is there any more, or is that it? No brains? No physical prowess? No special talents of any kind? No money to take you out and give you a good time? No job? No sex appeal? No rating on the popularity poll. What do you see in him, Juniper? Some spineless jerk who jumps every time you pull the strings?"

Juniper didn't reply, and he looked at her, surprised. She was leaning forward, her hands gripping the dashboard, her faced streaked with tears.

Kingsley swore and drove on, bitter and enraged.

Dylan threw back the blankets and got out of bed. He felt restless and uneasy, and he couldn't sleep. Something seemed to be pricking all his nerves, and his thoughts raced frantically. He felt unbearably tense.

He went down the dark passage and out into the kitchen. There was a full moon, and the light poured in through the windows, hard and bright on the stainless steel bench and the grey linoleum floor. He didn't put the light on but found a glass and poured himself some water. He drank it slowly, looking out the window across the vegetable garden and up at the shining night.

"Dylan?" The kitchen light flicked on, and his father came in. "Can't you sleep, Dylan?"

Dylan blinked in the sudden light, shook his head, and moved to put the glass on the bench. He missed, and the glass shattered on the floor. He swore, and his father shook his head and got the brush and dustpan from the laundry.

"I'll clean it up," muttered Dylan irritably, taking them. His hands were shaking, and the glass pieces rattled in the pan as he swept them up.

"Are you all right?" asked Tom anxiously. "You look sick."

"I'm fine!" snapped Dylan, cutting his knuckles on a jagged edge. "Go back to bed, Dad. I don't need you breathing down my neck."

"I was only trying to help. Look, you're getting blood all over the place. Here, let me do it."

"I'll clean it up! Hell, can't I even have a glass of water without everybody getting upset?"

"Hey — hold on a minute! The only person upset around here is you. Calm down."

Dylan finished sweeping up the glass, opened the back door, and banged the brush and dustpan down in the back porch, between the sneakers and rubbish bags. He slammed the door shut again and locked it.

Robyn came into the kitchen, rubbing her eyes and grumbling. "Who's making all the noise?" she wailed.

"Nobody! Go back to bed!" yelled Dylan.

Tom put his arm around Robyn and ushered her back to bed. When he came back into the kitchen, Dylan was running the cold tap over his cut hand and staring out at the darkness, frowning. His face was white.

Juniper watched the white line in the centre of the road and braced herself as they came up to another bend. A road sign flashed by, warning motorists to slow down to forty. Kingsley was doing eighty. She said nothing but gripped the dashboard in front of her, her knuckles white. She saw the bend rush up to meet them; saw the headlights sweep the road, the metal edge, the white rail — then the car smashed through the barrier. She heard Kingsley swear and felt the world slide and lurch, and all was bushes and small trees and long grass tearing across the glass in front of her face. Then the car tilted steeply and slid, sinking down into a vast rushing blackness that shone suddenly a muddy green, lit weirdly by the headlights and filled with bubbles and horror and a deep, roaring, sucking sound.

Juniper covered her face with her arms, unaware of the agony in her chest or the crazy angle of her body suspended in the tilting car; unaware of Kingsley's voice telling her calmly what to do and not to panic; aware only that she was trapped under tons of raging water.

She started to scream.

Dylan leaned on the kitchen bench, staring out at the darkness, holding onto the bench as though a huge weight was pushing him from behind. There was sweat on his face, and he breathed in deep gasps, as if he were in pain and terrified.

He gave a cry: "Juniper!"

And then he covered his face with his arms, leaning forward over the running water and the swirl of blood in the sink, and he screamed.

19

A Special Friend

IT was two in the morning when Tom finally turned out the twins' bedroom light. He went into the kitchen and sat with Dylan at the dining table. Dylan was drinking a cup of tea, holding it in both hands, his eyes wide and staring into space. His face was ashen, and he still shook all over.

"Are you feeling a bit better now?" asked Tom gently.

Dylan nodded. "I'm sorry, Dad," he said hoarsely. "Is Mr Shirazi gone?"

Tom grinned. "Yes, thank God. And his dog. It made more noise than you did. Mrs Mucklejohn came over, too, to see what all the noise was about."

"Sorry."

"Don't worry about it."

"I still think something's wrong, Dad. I know it is. Maybe I should ring Kingsley's place."

"No way, son. You've already phoned the police, the hospital, the Ministry of Transport, and Marsha. That's enough. So far as we know, Juniper and Kingsley are late home, that's all." He lowered his voice and gently put his hand on Dylan's shoulder. "I think all the strain of the past few weeks has been a bit much, Dylan. It's been tough on all of us, but on you most of all. I'm sorry I never saw it before. I was so wrapped up in my own problems, I didn't see what all this was doing to you. You can't be responsible for the twins and running this home and doing your homework. I haven't really been fair on you. I'm sorry. I'll put an ad in the paper next week for a housekeeper."

"It's nothing to do with that, Dad." Dylan put the cup down and covered his face with his hands. "I think she's dead, Dad."

The phone rang, and Dylan froze. He looked as if he were going to pass out.

Tom answered it. "Hello? . . . Mrs Golding? . . . Yes . . . All right . . . I'll tell him. Thanks. Thanks for letting us know."

He hung up and sat beside Dylan again. "She's all right, Dylan. Their car went into a river on the way home. They got out all right. They're bruised and cut a bit, that's all, and shocked. Juniper's in hospital overnight for observation. She'll be home later today. You'll be able to see her then."

Dylan slumped forwards, his face buried in his

arms. Tom put his arm around his son's shoulder and held him for a long time.

Marsha opened the front door and gave Dylan a grateful smile and a hug. "I'm glad you've come, Dylan," she said. "She's been asking for you all day. She won't talk to anyone, won't even mention the accident. She's still in shock, and very faint and shaky."

He followed her down the passage and into the lounge. Juniper was sitting in one of the chairs, looking tired and vulnerable and afraid. When she saw Dylan she got up, painfully, and went over to him. He put his arms around her, and she rested her head on his shoulder, her arms about his waist, and wept. He looked over her dark hair and saw Kingsley.

He was standing by the windowseat, tall and dark against the light. "Hello, Dylan," he said.

Dylan's voice stuck in his throat and crimson flooded his face. He felt a fool standing there in front of Kingsley, with Kingsley's girl in his arms. He glanced at Marsha, pleadingly. She understood and sat down.

"I think maybe it's time you went, Kingsley," she said quietly. "You can't do any more for Juniper."

Kingsley didn't move but just stood watching Juniper and Dylan, a strange expression on his face.

Juniper didn't move, either, and Dylan's colour

deepened. He moved his hands to her shoulders and tried to end the embrace, but she clung to him. It seemed a long time before she released him, slowly, and stood back. He noticed a large bruise on her forehead, one on her chin, and several smaller bruises and cuts on her collar-bone. Her right hand was bandaged across the knuckles. She looked at him without speaking and wiped the tears off her face. Her hand shook.

"It's good to see you," he said gently. "Last night I thought you were dead."

"Marsha told me you rang an hour before the police did," she murmured. "You're a special friend, Dylan. The best."

He blushed again and glanced awkwardly at Kingsley.

Kingsley sighed, almost laughed, and started walking towards the door. He stopped just behind Juniper and said, "Well, I'll be going, then. I think I know where I stand. I haven't got a chance against someone who reads your mind and knows your feelings and suffers when you do. I'm sorry for last night. It was my fault, entirely. I'm sorry." He hesitated. She didn't move. He looked at her straight, resolute back and her dark, curly hair. "Goodbye, then," he said.

"Goodbye, Kingsley." Still she didn't move or look at him.

Kingsley glanced at Dylan, and a brief, bewildered expression passed over his face; then he went out. Marsha got up and followed him.

Juniper gave a sigh and went and sat on the sofa. "Sit here with me, Leonardo," she said. She looked incredibly tired and hurt.

He sat with her, sinking low into the soft cushions, and he thought of the time he first sat here beside her and spilled his gingerbeer. It seemed centuries ago. It was.

He reached out and took her hand, noticing that it was cold. "You were a bit hard on him, weren't you?" he asked. "He really cares about you, Juniper."

"He nearly killed me," she said, her voice small and high and despairing. "It was terrible, Dylan. I tried to get out and I couldn't. There was so much noise, so much water bubbling and thundering all around. It was like being buried alive. I thought, this is it. I'm going to die. I'm going to die in the worst possible way. I was held up by my seatbelt, and the car was tipping forwards into the mud. I tried to get back to open the door, but I couldn't. Kingsley said the force of the water outside would be holding the door shut, anyway. I tried to wind down the window, but he wouldn't let me.

"There was water coming in everywhere, through cracks around the doors and in the tops of the windows and in the dashboard. He kept saying over and over again that we'd be all right, that if we waited until the car was nearly full the pressure would be equal inside and out, and we could open the doors and get away. Dylan, it was awful. I was screaming, and he hit me. And I had to stay there and wait with all that water all around, and with more water coming in, and wait while it came up over my knees and over the seat, and up to my waist. And then the car tilted back again, with the weight of the water in it, and I had to sit with the water creeping in all the time, and I could see the headlights shining through it outside, and it was muddy and filthy and there were eels and weeds and rotten trees.

"And then, when the water was up to my shoulders, Kingsley said we both had to take a deep breath and he'd open his door and we'd both go out that way, and he'd help me up to the surface. He said we had to stay together because it was dark and if we lost each other . . . Oh, Dylan. I was so frightened. He said we had to take a deep breath because he didn't know how far down we were. But I started to cry, and I couldn't breathe, and he dragged me out, and we went up through all that water and the slime and the blackness and the roaring, and it was hell, Dylan. I couldn't stand it anymore, and I took another breath. And there was water in my mouth and I breathed it in, and there was so much pain I thought I was going to die. There was so much pain."

She wept then, and Dylan put his arms around her and held her.

"The next thing," said Juniper, between sobs, "I was lying in the darkness in the grass, and Kingsley was breathing over my nose and mouth, and I wanted to be sick. I pushed him off, and I vomited up a whole lot of water. He said I hadn't been breathing for a while, and he was crying and said he thought I had drowned. I was so angry with him. I wanted to hit him, but I couldn't even stand up. And it was dark. We were still on the edge of the water, and my legs were in the river, and I was cold. So cold. I could see the car lights under the water, quite a long way up the river from us. Then some people came along the bank with a torch, and they helped us. They took us to hospital. I was so cold, Dylan." Her voice was calm now, her breathing regular, and she no longer wept.

After a while she groaned and sat up straighter, moving out of Dylan's embrace. "Sorry," she said, with a weak smile. "I've got bruised ribs. You can't hold me too tight."

He removed his arm, carefully. "I'll just have to love your mind, then," he said.

"My mind's a bit of a mess at the moment."

He grinned. "Join the club. Mine's a mess all the time."

She smiled, but her eyes were serious. "No it's not, Dylan. There's nothing wrong with you. You're the best human being I know." And she leaned towards him and kissed him on the mouth. He moved away after a while, his glasses steamed over, his breathing uneven.

"You shouldn't be doing things like that," he protested, taking his glasses off. "You've got damaged ribs."

"I'm perfectly all right from the neck up."

"I thought you said your mind was a mess."

"It's getting clearer all the time."

He smiled and gave her a tender and joyful look, then kissed her again.

20

Thanksgivings

ARSHA finished preparing dinner, then looked in the lounge again. Juniper was still sound asleep, lying on her back on the lounge floor, one arm flung across her face. She had been lying in a patch of sunlight earlier, but now it was evening and the room was dim with purple shadows.

Marsha left Juniper to rest and went upstairs to the attic. Dylan was sitting on the windowseat, looking at the picture he'd been working on for the past few hours. The attic, too, was purple and dim, but the sun's last rays slanted in, narrow and brilliant, shafts of liquid gold across Dylan's head and hands, and on the picture at his feet.

He looked up. "Hello, Marsha. Would you like to see what I've been doing?"

"I'd love to."

He picked up the portrait and held it in the light. "It's not quite finished yet," he explained. "I've got to finish the pencilwork in their clothes and the wood around the window, and do a bit more painting."

Marsha looked at the picture, and the strangest feelings flooded over her. She sat down slowly, smiling, though her eyes were moist.

"She's like a living soul," she murmured after a while. "There's something powerful about her, something alive and real. It's as if at any moment she's going to move or speak. She's beautiful, Dylan. Absolutely beautiful."

"Thanks." Dylan smiled and placed the portrait on the floor at their feet. The light slanted across it, brilliant on Johanna's face. Her eyes were like blue pools, clear, shining, and fathomless. He had finished painting her face and the child's, and there were faint touches of colour in the bowls of berries on the windowsill and in the bunches of herbs drying on the far wall. The finished pencilwork was detailed and finely done and almost photographic.

"How do you do it?" Marsha asked in a low voice. "Surely the images Juniper sends aren't this clear. They can't be. If this was something she saw once in a film, she couldn't possibly have remembered all the details. That's rue and sage drying on the wall, and those seed-heads are coriander. Those berries soaking in the wine are juniper berries. It's all so authentic, so real. She can't possibly have recalled it all; she doesn't even know those herbs."

She looked at Dylan and saw the colour rising in his face.

"You'd better tell me," Marsha said. "The truth. All of it. What's she been doing?"

Dylan took a deep breath and didn't dare look at Marsha's face. "Juniper doesn't send me scenes from films," he said hesitantly. "She meditates and goes through time and sees these people and these places."

Briefly, he explained Juniper's theory about the non-existence of time and her belief in the eternal Now. He mentioned Einstein's theory about time, and Carl Jung's revelation of the collective unconscious. All the time he talked, Marsha said nothing, but her face was drained and white.

"So I don't really know whether she travels through time," Dylan finished, "or whether she moves into that great pool of wisdom, and within that touches Johanna's spirit or her memories. But whatever she does, it's a real experience. And it's beautiful."

"Johanna?" said Marsha, faintly, her eyes on the portrait. "You even know her name?"

"What Juniper does, what she sees, is real. It's experienced with all our senses — our sight, smell, hearing. Everything except touch. We don't feel heat or cold or our surroundings. It's as if some senses are heightened and others are closed down. As if we're not there totally in our physical bodies but more in mind and spirit. And yet Johanna saw Juniper. I can't really explain it. I just know that it happens and that it's real. In the church Juniper overheard an old woman talking, and she mentioned Johanna's name. And her husband's called Edmund."

"You see and hear all of it, too?" asked Marsha. "It's not only a picture floating around in your head that you draw?"

He smiled and nodded. "I live it, too. That's what's so marvellous about it, Marsha. When Juniper sends me the images, it's all there, entire and perfect. Even the smells and sounds. And it doesn't stop just because she stops meditating and I stop drawing. I can still see Johanna in my mind as clearly as I can see you. I can see the sun shining on her hair, and the light in her eyes, and smell her herbs and kitchen fire, and see her clothes move as she breathes — "

"Oh, stop it!" Marsha cried, half laughing, afraid. "You're as bad as Juniper! You'll be telling me next that you sit and have coffee with these people."

"Not coffee," he said. "Hippocras, maybe." He grinned at her startled face. "Only joking, Marsha. We're not allowed to contact them or disturb them in any way. There are rules."

"And who told you the rules? Moses?"

"Vincent Gilroy. We told him what we're doing."

"That's a relief, then," she sighed, standing up. "I'm glad someone's keeping an eye on your endeavours."

He stood with her and put away the drawing. As they were going downstairs he asked: "Are there any other telepathic people in your family? What about Juniper's father? Did he have ESP?"

"I don't know," said Marsha, tripping on a stair and almost falling. She stopped on a small landing, a dark tapestry on the wall behind her, and she gave Dylan a strange, sad look.

"I didn't know her father," she said in a low voice. "I didn't even find out his name until I heard it in the courtroom. But out of all the humiliation and rage and suffering, Juniper came. And she's the best thing in my life. But there's a lot about her background and her that I don't know, and a lot of questions I'll probably never know the answers to. I think that's why you're good for her, Dylan: you're on the same wave-length with all this telepathic thing. She was a solitary soul until you came."

For a while Dylan said nothing. What she had told him disturbed him deeply, and saddened and angered him. At last he came to terms with it and looked at Marsha and gave her a slow smile. "Juniper's the best thing in my life, too," he said. "But I don't believe she was lonely. She's got more friends than anyone else I know. She's easily one of the most popular people in the school. All the guys think she's terrific."

"I didn't say she was lonely," said Marsha, "I said she was solitary. Alone. There's a difference. A person can have a lot of friends, but no one who truly understands them. It takes someone special to do that. And it takes time."

"Well, Juniper and I have got plenty of that,"

180

Dylan said, walking on down the stairs. "We've got centuries."

Marsha laughed and went out with him to the kitchen. "Set the table for dinner, please," she said, "and then go and wake up Sleeping Beauty and tell her to get that hippocras she made. That was a thirty-dollar bottle of my best red wine. We're all going to try it, even if it makes us sick."

Dylan leaned back in his chair, sighed contentedly, and pushed away his dessert plate. "That was fantastic, Marsha," he said. "I haven't eaten like that since Mum left."

"It's just as well," said Juniper, smiling at him over the rim of the silver chalice. "If you ate that much every night, you'd end up looking like Henry the Eighth."

He grinned and held out his hand for the chalice. "My turn with that, lady," he said. "You've drunk nearly that whole cupful. The rest's mine."

"You said you didn't like it," she said, handing him the chalice.

"I don't. It's horrible. But someone's got to drink it, and Marsha thinks it's poison, and you're still in shock and supposed to be taking things easy. That doesn't mean getting drunk."

"Speak for yourself, Dylan," said Marsha, getting up and beginning to clear the table. "You're cross-eyed. I'm taking you home later. You're not going on your bike."

"I'm perfectly sober," he choked hoarsely, finishing the hippocras. He placed the chalice on the table between himself and Juniper. "This stuff would probably do you a powerful lot of good if you had a cold," he said. "I bet that's why they used to drink it; it chased off plague. I bet Johanna never got the plague if she drank stuff like this. I wonder what she did die of."

"Childbirth, probably," said Marsha over her shoulder. "It wouldn't have been old age, anyway, Dylan. It seldom was in those days."

Dylan glanced at Juniper and saw that she was leaning forward on the table, pale and intense. He took her hand and felt that it was cold.

"What's wrong?" he asked anxiously. "Do you feel faint again?"

She shook her head and tried to smile. But her fingers folded around his, gripping his hand until it ached and his fingers went white and numb. He was about to say something when she let him go and stood up.

"Let's do the dishes," she said, and went out to the kitchen.

Dylan stood up slowly and flexed his hand. He stared after Juniper, frowning and bewildered. Then he picked up the chalice and a few more dishes and followed her out to the kitchen.

Juniper was relaxed again, giggling over a silly joke with Marsha, and piling dishes and cutlery into the soapy water in the sink. There was a knock on the door, and Dylan went to answer it.

It was Niall, looking tense and unshaven. He was breathing hard, as if he had been running. "Is she all right?" he asked.

"Yes. She's fine. Come in."

Niall hurried down the passage, almost running, and burst into the kitchen. He went up to Marsha and put his arms around her and almost wept. "I've been worried sick!" he said into her hair. "I've been trying to reach you all day. I had visitors until midday. Then the motorbike wouldn't start, so I walked to the public phone box and found it was out of order. The shop out there was closed, so I walked. Are you all right?"

Marsha drew away from him, her hands on his chest, and kissed his cheek. "Of course I'm all right. You walked? Twenty kilometres? Why?"

"I wanted to see you. I thought something was wrong."

Dylan glanced across the kitchen at Juniper, and she gave him a small smile and turned back to the dishes.

"Everything's fine now," Marsha told Niall. "But last night it wasn't. You walked?"

He grinned, inexpressibly relieved, and kissed her. "Crazy, aren't I?"

"Absolutely," she smiled.

"God, I love you, Marsha! I'd die if anything happened to you." He kissed her again, fervently, and Marsha pulled away.

"Not in front of the children," she said. "Let's leave them with the dishes, and we'll talk in the lounge."

They went out, their arms still about each other, and Juniper grinned and threw a tea towel at Dylan. "Do something constructive, Leonardo, instead of standing gawking," she said. "Unless you're learning something. Not that you need to. Your kissing's perfectly adequate."

He picked up a plate and dried it slowly. He looked crushed.

"Adequate," she said again, softly, smiling at him, "and warm, and inspiring, and terrific. You're beautiful, Dylan Pidgely. Why are you always so unsure of yourself?"

He put the plate down and picked up another. "Sometimes I think you're laughing at me," he said. "It's you I'm not sure of, not myself."

She sighed and turned her attention to the glasses in the sink. "I haven't been fair to you, have I, Dylan?" she said.

"No."

She was taken aback, and for a few minutes said nothing. He carried on drying the dishes, confused and self-conscious. He wished he hadn't drunk so much hippocras. His lips felt numb, and the room was blurred. Then he realised it was just his glasses steamed up.

"Have I hurt you awfully, Dylan?" She sounded as if she were crying, but he didn't dare look at her.

"Yes, you have," he said and was amazed that he said it.

"Why have you put up with me, then?"

"Because I love being with you. I love what we do, where we go. You're the only good thing in my life, Juniper. The best thing that's ever happened. What I have with you is gold, pure gold. Everything else is grey." All that amazed him, too.

Juniper bent over the sink, fishing for the knives and forks. "I'm sorry," she said, so quietly that he could hardly hear it.

He leaned down to kiss her cheek and kissed her hair instead.

"Don't apologise," he said. "Just come with me to the school social on Friday night."

She looked up, startled, and he saw that her cheeks were wet. Slowly, she smiled. "All right, Dylan Pidgely," she said, "I will."

For a moment he was stunned. The plate he was drying slipped from his hands and smashed on the floor.

"Will you?" he croaked. "Will you really?"

She laughed at the shock and terror and joy on his face. "Of course I will," she said. "Weren't you serious?"

"No — Yes. Oh, God. Yes."

Her smile widened. "Liar," she said.

But he had turned away and was giving a wild, un-Dylan-like whoop of triumph, when his elbow brushed the bench and another plate went crashing to the floor. Suddenly he caught her up in a great hug and danced her around and around the kitchen floor, soap bubbles and water and broken crockery flying everywhere. She cried out with pain, and he remembered her bruising.

"Sorry," he murmured, holding her suddenly as if she were made of the finest porcelain. He waltzed her around slowly, with infinite tenderness, and she laughed and went along with him, even though it hurt.

Marsha came in, took one look, and went out again.

"What's got into them?" asked Niall, looking at Marsha's amused face.

"Hippocras," she said.

"Hippo — what? Hippos again?"

"No. Hippocras. Medieval spiced wine." She sat down beside him again and smiled. "Don't worry, Niall," she said. "What they do is beyond me, too."

Things were quiet in the kitchen for a while, and then there were sounds of dishwashing being resumed, and quiet giggling, and broken crockery being swept up. After a while Dylan and Juniper came into the lounge, bringing coffee for everyone.

"It was fun doing the dishes?" Marsha asked, taking her cup from Dylan.

"Marvellous," he said. "We had a smashing time."

He gave Niall his coffee, then sat on the sofa by Juniper and slopped his own drink all down his jeans.

"I'm not getting up again," Juniper sighed. "You can go and get a cloth yourself."

"Doesn't matter, I'll wash them tomorrow." He looked in his cup. "I've still got a bit left to drink."

"You're improving, then," she said with a stunning smile.

*   *   *

Soon after supper, Dylan said he was going. Marsha wanted to drive him home, but he insisted on taking his bike. As he was leaving, Juniper called to him from one of the upstairs balconies.

"Romeo!"

He stopped his bike by the kerb and looked up. Her face was pale and shining against the ivy and the dark wood.

"What?" he called back.

She leaned over the balcony and called, in a voice low and passionate: " 'Good night, good night! Parting is such sweet sorrow that I shall say good night till it be morrow.' "

"I'm not waiting till tomorrow!" he shouted. "I'm tired."

"Will you two be quiet!" hissed Marsha from a nearby window. "Don't encourage her, Dylan. Go home."

"I can't!" he said, in a loud whisper. "It's Juliet. I think I'm supposed to climb up and kiss her." And he got off his bike.

"Don't you dare!" cried Marsha. Then she lowered her voice. "Go back inside, Juniper. You'll wake the whole neighbourhood."

"It won't hurt them to have a bit of culture," Juniper replied. She turned back to Dylan. " 'Art thou gone so, love — lord, ay, husband, friend! I must hear from thee every day in the hour —' "

"That's enough!" cried Marsha.

"Were they married?" yelped Dylan, surprised.

187

"Of course," said Juniper. "They had one whole beautiful night together."

"I'm glad the play had a happy end," said Dylan, getting on his bike again, and pedalling off.

"It didn't!" Juniper cried after him. "They killed themselves!"

But he didn't hear. He turned and blew her a kiss, nearly falling off his bike. She laughed and he went on, wobbling, not looking back again.

He enjoyed the ride home. The night was clear, warm, and full of silver light. He was thankful for every minute of the day, thankful for Juniper's life, for her laughter and her tears.

From now on, he thought blissfully, everything's going to be marvellous.

But that night the dreams began.

21

Dreams

OHANNA'S child ran along the narrow winding path between the trees, waving his arms as if he flew, and chirping to himself. In and out of sunlight he ran, the light glancing off his fair hair and flashing on his blue leggings and brown coat. He stopped in a patch of sunshine and inspected a plant with soft feathery leaves and yellow flowers, which was almost as tall as himself. He picked one of the flowers and sniffed it, his nose wrinkling, then he ran on. "Mother!" he called in a high, excited voice.

Johanna and Edmund were standing under a tree, talking, their hands linked. They looked up as the child approached, watching him with pleasure.

"A flower, Mother!" he cried, giving it to her. Johanna knelt in the grass and took the flower from the child's hands. " 'Tis rue, the herb of grace," she told him. "Be careful with it, love, it will hurt your hands and make your skin raw. But it is good for keeping bugs and fleas away, and to stop a cough. And if we rub the leaves on the floors at home, then any witches who come in must fly out again, and we will be safe."

The child threw his arms around her neck, laughing, and ran off again.

Johanna stood and leaned against the tree, watching him running through the light, her face dreaming and still. She was wearing a high-waisted plain gown, the same deep emerald as the trees. Her hair was unbraided and loose, and tangled with leaves and flowers that Edmund had threaded there.

He leaned beside her, his left hand on the tree beside her head. With his right hand he gently tilted up her face, and kissed her.

"I love thee well, wife," he said softly. "If any evil should befall you, my heart would break with grief."

"There's none that will befall," she replied, smiling, "and thy heart is strong."

" 'Tis only strong because you live," he murmured, kissing her again. When he lifted his head, his hazel eyes were disquieted, his face grave. "There are things they say of you," he said quietly.

She gazed up at him, her incredible eyes filled with laughter and light. "What things, love?"

"They say — they say that when you curse a

man, he is afflicted with illness or some other calamity. They say you do make poisons for old maids and love potions for the young. They say — "

"They say words more empty than the wind," she said. " 'Tis nothing, love. Nothing, and less than nothing."

"The wind is nothing yet powerful," he said. He hesitated a moment, then asked: "You make no poisons?"

"No."

"Gather no poisonous plants?"

"No, I swear! My herbs are for good, to flavour your stews, my lord, and to make pork more palatable when it has hung too long. And my rosemary sweetens the straw beneath our feet, and lavender sweetens our bed. How can you doubt?"

He sighed and bent his head towards her again and looked for a long time into her eyes. Slowly he smiled.

"You have an angel's eyes," he said, "and an angel's lips, and an angel's heart. If you have any power more than mortal power, then 'tis from heaven."

"Ay, it is," she smiled. "All light, and mercy, and love."

Their child came back, bringing bunches of wild flowers, and he dropped them at their feet and ran off again.

The air brightened; became so dazzling and intense that Johanna and her husband were lost in it. For a moment longer Juniper saw their forms;

heard him say something else and Johanna laugh, the sound joyous and radiant; and then she woke up.

For a long time she lay perfectly still, holding within her everything the dream had been — all the light and the bright laughter and the love. She wanted it to go on forever, to be always this shining, this perfect.

After a while, smiling to herself, she turned over and went back to sleep and had another dream.

She was in a long corridor, and at the end of it she could hear the sound of human voices shouting, and things being broken, and the high, piercing sound of a child screaming. Juniper struggled to wake herself, to draw back, away from the sounds; but the darkness sucked her under, caught her up, and swept her along towards the screaming and the shouts and the fury.

She saw Johanna's kitchen. Edmund, distraught, was tearing her bunches of herbs off the walls and flinging them into the fire. The child wailed and screamed and dragged at his father's cloak.

"And this!" Edmund cried, snatching up her straw broom that leaned against one wall and breaking it into pieces across his knee. Those, too, he flung violently into the flames, as he yelled at the child to leave.

The nurse came in and shrieked at Edmund to be calm. But he went on raging and shouting and burning Johanna's things, sweeping his arms along the table, scattering plants and spoons, and sending pottery and pewter crashing to the floor. The pottery bowls and cups shattered, but the pewter spun and rolled on the stones, ringing.

"She never told me!" Edmund cried, turning on the nurse. "She lied! I asked her, I did beg her, to tell me all the truth — and she did lie to me. Me — her husband and her truest friend! And now they have her, and she's being tried."

" 'Twas nothing evil, lord," the nurse said, hiding the child's face in her apron and covering his ears with her hands. "She made medicines, that's all."

"And you knew — and you told me not?"

"Lord, I — "

"Then out! Out! You're as in the wrong as she! Oh, Johanna! Johanna, my love! What have you done?"

He turned to the table again, picked up another handful of wilted leaves, and flung it furiously into the fire. He swept the glass bowls off the windowsill, spilling the wine and purple berries and sending the precious glass shattering on the street outside. The nurse fled, taking the child with her.

Last of all Edmund picked up the silver goblet. He stared at it for a few moments as if it were a foreign thing and hateful; then he slowly sank to his knees, his elbows on the wooden table, the chalice still in his hands. He turned it over and over, staring at it with fear and agony and love, then he bent his head into his arms and wept.

The hoarse, anguished sound of his weeping followed Juniper all down the darkness out of the chaos and the dream; followed her all through her waking, and through the long, terrible hours of the rest of that night.

When Marsha went in to see if she was well enough for school, she found Juniper sitting upright in bed, the chalice in her hands, staring at the portrait of Johanna as one would stare at a friend condemned to death.

Tom plastered a generous layer of marmalade across his toast and glanced at Dylan. "Not eating this morning?" he asked. Then he grinned. "Too excited, eh? I bet you'll be at the head of the queue, buying your tickets for that social. Your first official date. So old Kingsley's been given the boot at last. About time she made her mind up and decided who was the better man."

"It wasn't like that, Dad," said Dylan in a low voice. Last night's exultation had dissolved in a feeling of dread, which even his father's good humour couldn't alleviate.

"Well, I reckon it's time we all met this girl of yours," went on Tom, unaware of Dylan's mood. "Why don't you bring her home here for dinner before you take her to the social?"

"No. No, I'd rather not," muttered Dylan.

"She might get sick if she eats his cooking," giggled Barbara.

"I'll cook instead," offered Robyn generously. "I'll make pancakes. We made those at school. They were good, too, 'cept that the innards fell out."

Dylan stood up and put his empty cup on the bench. He went to the bathroom and cleaned his teeth, then went into his room and closed the door.

For a long time he gazed at the portrait of Juniper, and every moment his apprehension deepened. Yet he knew his fear was not for her; it was for someone connected with her. Johanna, he thought. No, that was ridiculous. He shrugged, denying the feelings altogether, piled his homework into his schoolbag, and went back to the kitchen.

His father had already left for work. The twins were still sitting at the table, their faces smothered with marmite and jam, pouring themselves second helpings of cornflakes.

"You haven't got time for that!" cried Dylan, clearing away their plates. "Go and get ready for school."

"I'm still starving!" wailed Robyn. "Give it back!"

"No. We're leaving in ten minutes. It'll take you that long to clean up your face. Go."

Grumbling loudly, they got down from the table and went down the passage to the bathroom. He heard them trailing their marmite fingers all along the walls. He sighed and started clearing the table. Suddenly he stopped and went over to the phone. He dialled Juniper's number.

Marsha answered.

"Hello, Marsha," he said. "It's me. Is everything all right?"

"Hello, Me," she replied, sounding tired. "No,

it's not all right, actually. Juniper's been having nightmares all night. She's not out of them yet, even though she's awake."

"What do you mean?"

Marsha sighed, and for one crazy moment he had the feeling that she was blaming him. "You've got this medieval thing all out of control, Dylan. She's totally confused. She's convinced Johanna is on trial. Now. She thinks they're torturing her or something. She says Johanna's husband is crying and burning all the evidence, but he ought to leave the house and take the child with him or they'll be forced to testify against her."

"How's she coping? Juniper, I mean."

"I know who you mean, Dylan. She's not coping at all. The doctor's coming soon. He'll have to give her a sedative or something."

"Do you want me to come around?"

"No. I think it's best if you stay away today. For a few days, maybe."

"Why?"

Barbara came screaming into the kitchen, swooped on her packed lunch, tore around the table like a miniature jet, and took off again. As she left, her schoolbag caught a corner of the tablecloth and she swept the whole thing off the table. Milk, cornflakes, cutlery, plates, and glassware all went crashing to the floor.

There was a stunned silence.

"Whoops," said Barbara, gazing at the mess. Then she giggled and fled.

"What on earth was that?" asked Marsha.

"One of the twins," muttered Dylan between clenched teeth. "I've got to go, Marsha. I'll phone again later. Goodbye."

He wasn't fast enough, and by the time he got to the front door the twins were already out the gate and gone. He swore and went back to the kitchen to start cleaning up.

But something in Marsha's voice had alarmed him. He felt even more afraid and apprehensive . . . but not for Johanna or Juniper.

That night Juniper dreamed again. This time it was about her own accident. She lived again the struggle with Kingsley up through the crushing darkness to the surface; she relived the fight, the terrible panic for air, and the agony of giving in to a world without it.

She woke up choking, sobbing with terror and pain.

Four kilometres away, Dylan sat bolt upright in bed, fighting to breathe. He clawed at the walls, suffocating, and felt only the overwhelming violence of the water rushing across him, filling his eyes and nose and mouth.

Tom shook his shoulders hard, and the force of the shaking woke Dylan. He leaned against his father, choking, drawing his breath in long painful sobs.

Tom sat beside him, bewildered and shocked, feeling his son's fearful shivering and his pyjamas damp with sweat. "It was a bad dream," Tom comforted him gently. "It's over now. You're all right."

Dylan nodded and wiped his pyjama sleeve across his face. "I dreamed I was in the car when it went into the river," he said shakily. "It was awful, Dad."

Tom nodded and looked up. The light from the passage came in through the open door, and Tom noticed the twins standing there, wide-eyed and alarmed. He went out to them.

"Your brother had a bad dream," he explained. "Go back to bed, now."

But Barbara pulled back, staring in fear into Dylan's room. "He's torn all the wallpaper," she whispered.

"He was dreaming," said Tom, taking them to their room and tucking them back into their beds.

Dylan looked at the wall beside him, then at his hands. Bloodied strips of wallpaper hung from his fingers, and several of his nails were bleeding, torn almost in half. Only then did he notice the pain.

He got out of bed and walked unsteadily to the bathroom, where he washed his hands. It was crazy, but he felt almost afraid of the water in the taps. He let out only the merest trickle and washed the blood off his nails. Glancing at his face in the bathroom mirror, Dylan saw that he was paper-white and his hair was damp.

He was putting sticking plasters on his damaged nails when his father came in. Tom sat on the edge of the bath, frowning and thoughtful.

"Forgive me if I'm being stupid," said Tom,

"but is it possible that she's dreaming all this, and you're picking it up from her?"

"That's what it is," said Dylan, straightening up and watching the blood seep out around the edges of the plasters. "And I don't know what to do about it, Dad."

"You'll have to think of something," said Tom. "Kathy was in a bad accident just before I met her. She wasn't seriously hurt, but she was still having nightmares about it a year later."

Dylan glanced at his father, horrified. "Poor Juniper," he said.

"Poor you, too, if you have to go through it with her," said Tom. "There's something I want to say to you, Dylan. Something that has to be said. I'm not sure that Juniper's good for you. No — let me finish. I know you love being with her, but she seems to have a disruptive influence on your life. When you're with her, everything else flies out the window. I don't understand what you two have got going between you, but I guess it's something telepathic. Am I right?"

Dylan nodded but said nothing. His face had gone hard, and he looked defensive.

"Well," Tom went on carefully, "I think it's not healthy to have such a strong bond between you. If you want to stay friends with her, you've got to learn where to cut the feelings off."

"She's not disruptive!" cried Dylan angrily. "I know I got pretty tied up there once. I know if I hadn't been so involved at her place, I'd have seen what Mum was going through, and I'd have been at home that day instead of at Niall's, and she'd never have gone. I know all that's my fault. But there's nothing — "

"I didn't mean all that," said Tom gently. "I've told you you're not to blame, that nothing's your fault. You're tormenting yourself for nothing, son. Your mum left because I was seeing Evelyn — not because you didn't come home that day she wanted you to. I'm just concerned that Juniper's influence on you is rather strong, that's all. And I feel helpless because I can't do anything to help you. I haven't even met her. But you're going to have to learn how to control her influence, how to stop the feelings."

"That's up to her," said Dylan, going back to his room.

Tom sighed and followed him. He stood for a long time in Dylan's doorway, watching his son. Dylan was back in bed, sitting up, a book across his knees. He obviously had no intention of going back to sleep if he could help it.

"What do you mean, it's up to her?" asked Tom.

Dylan turned a page. "Just that, Dad. She sends the images, I receive them. That's the way it is. I haven't got any say in it. It's not as if there's a blind I can pull down to shut it all out."

"Well, there ought to be," said Tom heavily, as he went out and closed the door.

22

Borderlands

HE dream started even before Juniper was wholly asleep, and she was aware in her conscious mind of the dragging darkness and the roaring tumult of the waters. Desperately she fought to wake herself, to lift her head off the pillow and force her eyelids to open. But the water was in her eyes and in her nose and mouth, smothering her, and she felt Kingsley's arms holding her, binding her, forcing her up through the never-ending blackness, and she fought to be free, fought with all her strength; then, when she could bear it no longer, she opened her mouth and breathed in . . .

Then she was on the bank again, choking and gasping down great lungfuls of sweet air, and Kingsley was bending over her, saying something, but his hands on her face were rough, and when his fingers dragged her hair from her eyes she saw it was daylight, and Kingsley was not crying from grief, but his face was twisted and ugly with rage and hate, and unrecognisable. With a shock she realised it wasn't Kingsley at all, but a man with coarse woollen leggings, a green wide-sleeved coat, and long unwashed hair. Terrified, she looked beyond him and saw a whole crowd of people, women and children in long dresses with white caps on their heads, screaming and pointing at her with hatred and fear; and a group of dark-robed priests, quiet and gloating and triumphant.

She screamed and tried to get up to run, but she was bound tightly hand and foot and could only lie there, helpless. She turned her head aside, away from their faces and accusing hands, and saw that the houses across the water were ancient and made of stone, and the hair across her face was long and straight and the colour of corn.

She woke drenched with sweat, tore the sheet off her face, and reached frantically for the light. It was turned on for her, and Marsha leaned over her, loving and concerned.

"You cried out in your sleep, Juniper. You were dreaming again."

"Stay with me!" cried Juniper, clinging to her. "Don't let me go to sleep again. Talk to me, bring me cups of tea, give me something to do — anything, but don't let me sleep!"

Marsha stayed with her for an hour, and at last Juniper lay back on the pillows, dozing, her eyelids red from crying. Quietly, Marsha went out, but she left on a dim light.

A warmth flooded over Juniper; a bright, sweet, lovely warmth of sun and summer wind. When she opened her eyes she was gazing up at skies a clear and vivid blue. But someone was doing something to her feet. Strong cords were binding her ankles, and she could feel her legs being bound tightly, to the point of pain.

She didn't move. She could hear a great crowd of people murmuring, but she didn't look at them. She felt her arms being tied behind her back, and the tension of the ropes made her shoulders and back ache. She could hear a man speaking, his voice reverent and low but very clear, and was aware of the crowd falling silent, listening.

"May omnipotent God, Who did order baptism to be made by water, and did grant remission of sins to men through baptism; may He, through His mercy, decree a right judgement through that water."

The voice came closer, and a priest stood near her. She could see him out of the corner of her eye; could smell the incense from the church and see the herbs of protection fixed to his robes. She refused to look at him.

"If — " he said to her in the same calm, clear voice, "if thou art guilty, may the water which received thee in baptism not receive thee now; if, however, thou art innocent, may the water which received thee in baptism receive thee now. Through Christ our Lord."

He turned away again, towards the river, and she knew that he sprinkled holy water over it, and exorcised it, and blessed it.

She tried not to listen and looked up at the brilliant skies where she saw a white bird flying high against the sun. She took it as a sign and smiled. But her arms and legs were throbbing already with pain, and the world blurred. She swayed and would have fallen, but someone steadied her. The priest's voice rose, still addressing the water, authoritative and full of power.

". . . in no manner thou receive this woman, if she be in any way guilty of the charge brought against her. And may no process be employed against thee, and no magic . . ."

The world faded again, and she was afraid she would faint. She took a deep breath, lifted her head and said a prayer. The person standing beside her laughed and spat. She heard the priest's Amen and then strong hands took hold of her. She could hardly breathe for fear, and the earth spun and the sky crashed down on her. She felt herself lifted; she was suspended, briefly, between heaven and earth, circling like the bird; and then the river took her, and the drowning began all over again.

The book slid out of Dylan's hands, and his head dropped back onto the pillow. He thought he heard voices, a whole crowd of voices, and dreamed he was on a bank beside a stream. He thought he was at Niall's and felt vaguely amused, wondering how Niall would cope with this huge invasion on his privacy. Then he realized it wasn't Niall's river, nor any place he knew. He saw the people and the priests and the woman being bound. And he knew, though her face was away from him, who she was. He watched, helpless and enraged, as they tied her; watched as the priest exorcised the water and prayed; watched as they lifted her and threw her in.

He saw her vanish in a swirl of water and saw the priests and the people rush to the edge, watching. He felt sickened and wanted to smash their faces. But though he was among them, he had no form, no flesh, no power. He saw her float to the surface, face down, and saw that her hands strained against the ropes, her fingers white and stretched. Slowly she rolled over, her hair across her face, and he could see her mouth open, hungering for air. The crowd roared and screamed, and he noticed Agnes there, and Maud, and several of Johanna's friends. But her friends were white-faced and stricken, and several of them prayed. He looked for Edmund and the child but couldn't see them.

When he looked at Johanna again she was rolling over in the water, helpless, her body convulsed. He looked away, anguished, willing her to die, to die quickly and without pain. But the priests were ordering several men into the water to pull her out.

"No!" he screamed, rushing at them. But they moved like wind before him, and in the water he felt nothing. And Johanna lay on the grass retching, her body wracked with sobs, and the people screamed for a burning.

He woke up shaking and hot and flung off the tangled bedclothes. He was panting as if he'd run a race, and sweat trickled down his back. He could hear Mr Shirazi's dog next door, barking like a mad thing. He switched on his light and got up.

He went out to the kitchen, switching on lights everywhere he went, and got himself a cold drink. The dog barked on and on, furiously, and Dylan put down his glass and listened. That dog hardly ever barked. Not usually. Still shaking, and feeling more and more apprehensive, Dylan unlocked the back door and went out.

The light from the kitchen window made a yellow patch on the lawn, and the moon was almost full. He could see Mr Shirazi's Alsatian over by the fence, outside its kennel, straining at the chain and growling horribly. Suddenly the chain broke and the dog took off. It raced around to the front of the house, and Dylan followed it. A light went on in the Shirazi's house and Dylan felt less afraid. He followed the dog out onto the road, calling to it, bewildered and angry.

The dog was standing in the centre of the road by the white line, barking and growling, all its hackles up. It circled an empty place on the road, frenzied.

"Come back, you great idiot!" Dylan yelled angrily. "There's nothing there!"

But the dog wouldn't move, so Dylan went

closer, suddenly cold and afraid. A shadow moved on the road; a sideways sliding of dark brown and a glimmering of white. He could make out a robe, a long dress of some sort, and the pale folds of a scarf, blue in the moonlight. He saw a face, old and bewildered and terribly afraid. It was Agnes. Agnes of Tewkesbury.

The dog went berserk, and Dylan threw himself on it, gripping its collar. He felt Agnes's dress brush his face and saw her shoe. Then she was gone. He knelt on the road by the dog, his head on its neck. The dog growled softly and wouldn't touch the place where Agnes had been.

Mr Shirazi came out in his pyjamas, holding a brass poker. His face looked alarmed and gaunt, his whiskers long and dark.

"What's going on?" he asked. "What's the matter with me dog? You Pidgelys causing trouble again?"

He took hold of his dog's collar and helped Dylan to his feet.

"It's nothing," Dylan muttered, turning away to go back inside.

"It's always nothing!" yelled Mr Shirazi. "That's what you said last time!"

Dylan's father was standing in the front porch, listening to all the yelling. "Was it a prowler, Dylan?" he asked.

Dylan shook his head and went into his room. He pulled on his jeans and a red shirt, though his fingers were shaking so much he could hardly do it up.

"What's wrong?" asked Tom, sitting on Dylan's tumbled bed, suddenly uneasy. "What was out there?"

"Agnes," said Dylan, his teeth chattering. "Old Agnes. I've had enough. I'm going to see Juniper."

"It's four in the morning!" cried Tom, alarmed. "You can't go visiting now!"

"Why not?" yelled Dylan, storming out the front door. "Everyone else is!"

"Who's Agnes?" asked Tom, following Dylan out to the garage.

Dylan hauled out his bike and got on. "You wouldn't understand, Dad," he said.

"Try me."

"All right. Agnes is one of the women who accused Johanna of witchcraft. She lived in Tewkesbury, in the fifteenth century."

Tom half laughed, then looked sick. "You're joking," he said.

"I wish I were," said Dylan, as he biked off.

Juniper sat up in bed, shaking and terrified, and looked at the portrait of Johanna. She could hear Edmund weeping again; could hear it even though she was fully awake and her hands were over her ears and she'd turned on her radio to distract herself. She heard him, and she heard their child. But from Johanna she heard nothing. Johanna would never speak, no matter what they did to her: Johanna had nothing to confess. So her husband wept, and the child wept, and Juniper wept, and someone banged on the front door, loudly.

Juniper heard voices downstairs; Marsha's raised and angry and Dylan's shouting. Moving slowly, as if a great heaviness weighed her down, Juniper got out of bed and put on some jeans and a loose shirt. She went into the bathroom and washed her face with warm water. She looked in the mirror, and was shocked at her dull, tormented eyes and her pale lips. "Oh, Johanna," she groaned, despairingly, "you've aged me twenty years in one night. God, what's Dylan going to think?"

But Dylan was too angry to notice.

"I've seen Agnes," he said, as soon as Juniper went into the lounge. "I've seen her. So has Mr Shirazi's dog. She was out on the road, outside my home. She was real, Juniper. I touched her gown when I stopped the dog attacking her."

Juniper groped blindly for a chair and sat down. She bent her head in her hands, her shoulders slumped, her whole being crushed. She could still feel the cords binding her and hear the crowd howling for her death. And above it all came Dylan's voice, cold and embittered and condemning.

"This has gone far enough!" he shouted. "There's no control anymore — no beginning, no end, no boundaries, no discipline, no peace. It's all mixed up. Where's the end, Juniper?"

He leaned over her and gripped her shoulders hard, forcing her to look at him.

"You're hurting," she said.

His face softened, and he bent his head against hers. "I'm sorry. I'm scared, Juniper. It's all got too powerful for us." He let her go and crouched on the floor in front of her, his arm across her knees, and looked into her face. He was shocked at the pain there.

"She didn't drown, Dylan," Juniper said, tears pouring down her face. "She lived. They're going to burn her. But the priests will torture her first and make her confess. They'll strip her and shave off all her hair and — "

"Hush." He put up his hand and pressed his fingers across her lips, gently. "They won't do anything," he said. "It's all been done. It all happened five hundred years ago, Juniper. Your soul's been travelling, and it touched what happened to Johanna, but it isn't living through it with her. It's finished. Whatever happened is over now. Johanna is dead and buried. Edmund's dead, too, and their child, and their grandchildren. Ages have passed. It's over."

"Then why was the dog attacking Agnes?" she asked.

Dylan sighed and bent his head. He couldn't answer.

"I'll tell you why," Juniper whispered. "It isn't over, Dylan. Because I was Johanna. They tried to drown me then and couldn't. And I was nearly drowned again, with Kingsley, and I lived. They burned me then, and I'll burn again. There'll be another car accident, or a house fire, or an explosion of some sort. I'll burn again. And then it'll be over, Dylan."

He shook his head. "You've got it all wrong,"

he said, speaking calmly but with deep conviction. "I've already told you. Your soul has touched hers, that's all. There's an understanding between you, a strong bond, because of the silver chalice, and all the things you love, and your soul sisterhood. That's all."

"Then why the near-drownings? Coincidence?"

"No. What's happening to us now is also outside Time, remember. In the eternal Now, near-drowning has always been in your life. Destiny knew that, foresaw it, long before you were born. So when your soul first touched Johanna's, your fear of water matched hers and strengthened the understanding between you. You both suffered the same thing. But there's no threat of fire in your life. You love fire and candles and light."

Juniper sighed and slumped back in the chair as if an unbearable weight had fallen from her.

"But it doesn't stop the pain," she said helplessly. "It doesn't stop the dreams or being stuck with Johanna in the place she is now. And right now she's being tried. And I'm in it with her, and I can't deny that or pretend it isn't happening."

"You two are going around in circles," said Marsha from behind them.

They'd forgotten Marsha. Dylan sighed heavily and stood up.

"I think it's time you went now, Dylan," said Marsha, her voice sounding strangely distant and cool. "Juniper's gone through enough. And it's five in the morning."

Dylan bent and kissed Juniper's cheek. It was wet and deathly cold. "I'll see you after school," he said gently. "I'll think of a way to see us through this place, I promise. There's a purpose in it, somewhere."

She nodded and almost smiled, but she looked like a person condemned.

He went out, hating to leave her. At the front door he stopped, puzzled. All his drawings were in the cardboard folder, propped up by the door. He checked through them quickly, bewildered. Even the unfinished portrait of Johanna was there, taken down from the wall in Juniper's room.

"I think you should take them away," said Marsha behind him.

He turned and faced her and saw that all her warmth was gone.

"They don't help Juniper," she said wearily. "They're what gives her the nightmares. Take them out of this house and never bring them back."

"I can't take them now," he said. "I came on my bike."

"Your bike's in the boot of my car. I'll take you home."

"I could have come back tomorrow and got my bike."

She said nothing but just stared at him, sad and unsmiling.

"You don't want me to come back, do you?" he said, and was amazed that he sounded so calm. Inside, he was in chaos.

"No. I'm sorry, Dylan. It's not you. It's what

you do. It's all right for someone to have dreams and visions, but when someone else sees those dreams, too, and draws them, it's like a confirmation, a bringing to reality. Juniper was all right thinking about medieval things, until you came and drew them."

"I was invited, remember."

"I also remember warning you and telling you to be careful to keep it under control."

"Is kicking me out your idea or Juniper's?"

"Mine. And I'm not kicking you out, Dylan."

"That's what it feels like."

"I'm sorry. Take the drawings to the car. Please."

They said nothing all the way to Dylan's home, except when he gave her his address and a few directions. When they arrived, Dylan got his bike out of the boot while Marsha took the folder of drawings and leaned it against the gate. Dylan stood with his bike, waiting for her to go. She hesitated, lingering by the gate, her face shadowed in the early dawn and distraught.

"I'm sorry, Dylan," she said brokenly. "It's not you, believe me. I think you're a fine person and the best friend Juniper's ever had. But I have to protect her."

"Against her own imagination and gifts?"

"I don't know, Dylan. There are so many things about her I don't know. I'm afraid for her. I'm afraid of all the things I don't know about her, of all the things I don't know about her father. I'm afraid of things she may have inherited from him, emotional and mental things. I have to protect her mind."

She wiped her hands over her face and couldn't speak anymore. She got into the car and drove away.

Dylan watched the red tail-lights vanish down the glimmering street and swore.

"Damn her father!" he cried. "Damn Agnes! Damn the whole bloody medieval justice system."

He wheeled his bike into the garage, went back for the folder of drawings, then went inside.

23

The Victors

OMEHOW, Dylan managed to survive the next three days. He didn't see Juniper — she wasn't at school — and she didn't phone, nor did he call her. Friday came, the evening of the school social, and Dylan sat at home and watched television with the twins before going to bed early.

As usual, he read until the small hours of the morning to keep the dreams at bay; but he had hardly closed his eyes when they began.

Mercifully, in a way, it was always only water and never flames. And yet he had come to long for the flames, knowing that then there'd be an end to it. Sometimes the dreams were of Edmund, sitting alone on a vast, high, curtained bed, weeping and mourning. Sometimes he was holding his son, and they sat in long anguished silences, and the boy looked confused and sometimes asked where his mother was. Once, Dylan saw old Agnes sitting on a stool in Johanna's kitchen, talking to the nurse. Agnes was saying things Dylan couldn't hear, but Johanna's son, playing by the fire, burst suddenly into tears, and the nurse held him and rocked him, but he wouldn't be comforted. And then Edmund came and roared something terrible at Agnes, and she fled out into the street.

Sometimes Dylan saw Johanna again, but she looked white and shocked, and all the light in her had died. And always the waters thundered across her and the river claimed and then rejected her, and the people clamoured for a burning.

On Saturday Dylan waited for the phone to ring, convinced that Juniper was trying to contact him; but it didn't, and late in the afternoon he went for a ride on his bike. He ended up away out at Richmond, at the site of the demolished factory he had once drawn. The factory was totally gone now, even the chimney had been toppled and taken away, and a new building was in progress. He stared at the high concrete walls, but the grey kept blurring, and the concrete looked like ancient stones, running with slime and damp. He had strange pains all over his body and a terrible heaviness of spirit.

He biked home in heavy rain, and had never felt more cold and abandoned and alone in all his life.

Tom sat by Dylan and handed him a cup of coffee. "Are the twins asleep?" he asked, and Dylan nodded.

They were in the lounge, and the rain still poured down outside, making a loud drumming sound on the iron roof and against the windowpanes.

Dylan looked exhausted and sad, and there were dark shadows about his eyes. He sipped his coffee slowly, gazing at the wall opposite and the print of the wide-eyed child crying.

"I had a phone call while you were out this afternoon," Tom said, smiling. "It was your mum. She's coming back."

Dylan went on sipping his coffee, his eyes still on the print. "That's great, Dad."

"Thanks for your wild enthusiasm. I thought you'd be pleased."

Dylan's eyes blurred, and he glanced at his father. A smile crossed his face, briefly, like a light, and was gone again. "I am pleased, Dad," he said.

"But you've got other things on your mind."

"Yes. When's she coming home?"

"She's catching a bus tomorrow. She'll be here for dinner. I won't tell the girls until after lunch, otherwise they'll be racing out to meet the bus every two minutes." Tom grinned. "We'll cook something really special. One of your lasagna dishes. And I'll make a dessert. We'll have a bottle of wine, too, to celebrate. I bought one today."

Dylan said nothing, and Tom sighed. "I wish I knew how I could help you, son," he murmured. "It's Juniper, isn't it?"

"Yes. I'm not seeing her again."

"I'm sorry. I know what you're going through. Believe me."

"She's the best person I know, Dad. My best friend. My only friend."

They were silent for a while, listening to the drumming rain.

"She didn't phone today, did she?" asked Dylan.

"No. I was here all afternoon. I cleaned up the house, in case you didn't notice. Your mum called, then one of Robyn's friends. No one called for you."

They fell silent again, and Tom sighed and finished his coffee. "You're a strange one, Dylan," he said. "You used to be predictable, always in your room with your head in a book or copying pictures of knights and horses and messing around with cardboard castles. Now you take off on your bike at four in the morning, mad as a meat-axe, and visit some girl I've never even met. And then you come home with some drawings that look like they're worth a million dollars and tell me that you did them. You never sleep, and your life's upside down. What's happened to you, son?"

Dylan gave him a wry sideways look and half smiled. "Juniper happened," he said.

* * *

The next day Dylan was in the kitchen, preparing the lasagna, when the twins came racing in, falling over themselves with excitement.

"Your girlfriend's here!" Robyn screamed, pulling on Dylan's arm and scattering pasta all over the floor.

"She's got lovely hair," sang Barbara, prancing across the pasta and running her hands through her short curls. "She's got hair like mine's going to be when I grow up."

Dylan watched them, paralysed, disbelieving.

Robyn leaned out the kitchen window and called to her father: "Dad! Come and see Juniper! She's beautiful!"

Dylan dropped the onion he was slicing and ran down the passage to the front door, skidding to a halt right in front of her.

She was smiling, though a deep anxiety showed in her eyes and her face was very pale.

"Hello, Dylan."

He stared at her, conscious of his hands smelling of onion and of his mother's apron tied around his waist. Slowly he put his arms around her neck and hugged her close.

"It's good to see you, Juniper," he said, his mouth against her hair. "God, it's good to see you."

"I phoned yesterday, but you were out. I talked to Robyn."

"She didn't say."

"I know. So I decided to come around. I hope you don't mind."

"No. No, of course not. Come in." He turned around and saw Tom and the twins behind him, watching. He blushed, one arm still around Juniper's neck, and introduced her.

"Juniper, that's my dad, Tom. And that's Barbara on the left, and that's — "

"I'm Robyn," said Robyn. "Does he kiss you?"

Tom put his hand on Robyn's shoulder, warningly, but Juniper laughed.

"Sometimes he does," she said, and Robyn giggled, delighted.

"I'll show you my dolls," said Barbara, grabbing Juniper's hand and pulling her down the passage towards her room. Juniper went with her, glancing helplessly back over her shoulder at Dylan, her lips curved. Robyn skipped after them, chanting something about Mrs Tiffany. They went into the twins' room, and Robyn slammed the door.

"Looks like you've lost her," Tom observed grinning. "At least they'll give you time to wash your hands and take off your apron. You'd better tidy your room, too, if you want to talk to her in private."

As Dylan raced off, Tom called him back. "Son? I'm proud of you. She's a beautiful girl."

"I know," said Dylan with a brilliant smile. "She's beautiful all through."

Five minutes later Dylan poked his head into the girls' room. Juniper was sitting between them on the floor, admiring their teddybears. She looked up, and Dylan saw the underlying uneasiness again, the grief and pain.

"Juniper and I are going to talk now," he said, and the twins howled and clung on to her.

"I'll see you before I go, I promise," said Juniper, struggling to her feet.

"Will you stay for dinner?" asked Robyn eagerly, pulling on her arm. "Please. Mum'll be here tonight, too. She's staying forever and ever."

Juniper glanced across at Dylan, and he smiled. "You're very welcome," he said, "if you want to risk my cooking."

"I'd love to," she said, laughing, and the twins cheered. They let her go, reluctantly, and Dylan took her into his room.

Miraculously, it was tidy. He just hoped his wardrobe door wouldn't fly open. "We can talk in peace in here," he said.

She looked around and saw the three pictures of Johanna. They were pinned up along one wall, and beside them was a small portrait of herself. She looked at all his books, crammed two layers deep in the makeshift bookshelves and spilling over into piles along the walls. She saw his homework table, hurriedly tidied but still chaotic. She noticed the torn wallpaper beside his pillow, the threadbare carpet, the flaking paint on the ceiling, and the cracked varnish on the doors. She saw all the things he'd hoped she'd never see, and he realised they meant nothing to her.

"You're my best friend, Dylan," she said in a

low voice. "When you walked out that last time, I felt utterly alone." She looked suddenly very tired, and she sat cross-legged on the floor, her head bent.

He said nothing but sat in front of her. They were both wearing jeans, and over the blue their hands crossed and held.

"Marsha's sorry," she said, looking up. "She wants — we both want — you to come to dinner tomorrow night. If you want to. She said to tell you she didn't mean what she said the other night. She was only doing what my doctor told her to. And what she thought was best for me."

"She knows you're here now?"

"She brought me in the car. She didn't stop to come in; she said she'll see you tomorrow. She said it was important that you and I talk. She thought that what we were doing was dangerous, Dylan. I think she was afraid I wasn't strong enough mentally to cope with it."

"What made her change her mind?"

"Niall. He told her the doctor didn't know what he was talking about. He said if anyone had the strength and the vision to see us through this, it was you." She smiled suddenly, and it was like a light breaking on her face. "Niall and Marsha are getting married."

"That's terrific!" He laughed, and they leaned towards each other and embraced.

Juniper drew away again and linked her hands with his. "I'm glad," she said. "Niall's the only man she's had that I can remember. He's good for her; helps her to laugh at things."

"Is he giving up his gypsy caravan, then?"

"Heavens, no! They'll go there for weekends and holidays and to get away from me every now and again." She grinned and squeezed his hands. "We'll be able to meditate all we want, and drink hippocras, and listen to loud music. I found a tape of Egyptian music the other day."

"I didn't know they had any."

"They had lots of things besides pyramids and hieroglyphics. I'll take you there sometime."

"Ancient Egypt?"

She laughed at the look on his face. "Why not? You don't think we're stopping at England, do you?"

"Oh God, Juniper! I can't keep up with you!"

"I thought you kept up with me very well. You're the only human being who has. What are you like at dancing?"

"No good at all. Why? Are we dancing in Egypt?"

"No. At our Fourth Form Christmas social. Will you come to that with me, since we missed the last one?"

He grinned, enormously relieved. "I'll dance anywhere with you, except in Egypt."

"Don't limit yourself, Leonardo."

"I have to. We've flown in some great places, Juniper — the highest and best places — but maybe there's danger in them, too. Maybe our wings aren't strong enough yet. Maybe there are limits — there have to be limits — or we'll be lost, overwhelmed. I'm not asking you to forget your visions of other times; only that you treasure them for what they are and don't allow them to become out of perspective with life now. Forget about Egypt, Juniper. We don't need it. Dance with me here, in the twentieth century. And let's finish our business with England."

Juniper sighed and gave him a small smile. "I suppose it has all got too much for us," she said. "But England's not over yet." She bent her head, all the suffering and shock rushing back, too strong to deny any longer. Dylan waited, saying nothing, while all her pain became his.

Slowly, Juniper lifted her head. She looked straight into Dylan's face and said simply, "They're burning her today."

"Not today," he said gently. "Thousands of todays ago."

"It's today. Today, Dylan. Today she stands tied to the stake, waiting. The wood's piled high all around, and a man is standing with a flaming torch, ready to set it alight. It's all slowed down, halted somehow, as if something waits.

"She's so alone, Dylan. Edmund's not there, her child's not there. Some of her friends are, but they're in the background, afraid to be associated with her anymore. She's wearing a horrible black robe, and they've shaved off all her hair, but she still looks lovely. And she's alone. She's suffered horribly. She doesn't know anymore whether she's right or wrong, good or evil. She's terrified that she is a witch, and she'll die and burn forever in some terrible medieval hell. She has no faith left, no hope, no friends. She thinks even God hates her. She's alone. Totally alone."

"Then we'll stand with her," he said.

Her eyes widened a moment, unsure, joyful, and half afraid. "Can we do that?" she asked.

"We have the power. There's nothing else we can do for her; we can't save her life or give her an easier death. But we can be with her. Maybe that's the purpose in all this: to help her in her dying."

Juniper gave him a slow, wondering, tender smile. "You're a special human being, Dylan Pidgely."

He said nothing, but, smiling, leaned across their clasped hands and kissed her. Then he bowed his head, his eyes closed, as if he sought already the place where Johanna was and knew in his own mind how to go there.

Juniper watched him for a few moments, then bent her head to his and went with him.

Dylan saw a calm summer sky, and under it a crowd of people all shouting and violent and filled with hate. He saw their mouths open, screaming, and some of the mothers held their children high to see better the dying of a witch. He saw their mouths open as they cried out, but all was deathly slow, the sounds muffled and drawn-out and dim.

He was aware of a single form, a woman in

black, to his right and slightly behind him; and of Juniper on her other side. He moved back until he stood beside her, and though the wood was packed in hard all around, he moved through it easily, as though it had no form. He looked at Johanna's drooping head and saw that her face was bloodless and strained, her eyes hollow and despairing. Her hair was a golden stubble and her wide cheekbones and pointed chin seemed finer still, clearer, and even more beautiful. A rough wooden cross hung on a leather thong about her neck.

He looked beyond her at Juniper, also white and strained but unafraid. He half smiled, and Juniper leaned across in front of Johanna and touched his hand. For a moment Johanna lifted her head, alert; and her eyes were filled suddenly with hope. Her gaze shifted, and she looked straight at Juniper.

And then the tumult of the crowd broke over them. The people shrieked accusations and curses; children screamed; and the man with the flaming torch stepped forward and set it to the waiting wood. There was the crackle of burning and the bitter smell of smoke. Johanna started to sob and to strain against the ropes. Then she looked at Juniper again, and stood tall and straight, and was calm.

Together, Dylan and Juniper covered her with light. They poured it over her, brilliant white and filled with all the shining things she loved. They held her in it there, and even when her clothes flamed and the fire raged and the smoke was choking black, their light was like a shield and a covering, and they held her there, high; and were beside her when she died.

Edmund leaned against the tree and watched his son at play. He was running along the winding path, waving his arms half-heartedly and making strange, mournful bird sounds. Soon he gave up and came back to his father.

"Mother Agnes said witches go to hell," said the child gravely. Then his face crumpled, and he started to sob. "She said when witches burn they go mad and scream curses and devils fly out of their mouths."

Edmund crouched in the grass and put his arms around his son. The boy leaned close, sobbing, and Edmund stroked his hair gently.

"Hush, Leonard," he said softly. "I will tell thee a thing passing strange and beautiful that has been all my comfort in these past weeks."

The child stopped crying and listened, his face against his father's chest.

"Your mother told me many times in those last months before they came for her that she did often feel a presence watching over her, strong and good. And once she saw a form, all covered in golden light, that came and smiled on her and went away again.

"And I will tell you this, too, Leonard, though your heart is young. Methinks you'll understand it better than I. When your lady mother died, some came to me later and said that she died all quiet and noble, like a queen. They said she was all covered

227

in light, unearthly and shining. And some said white birds flew around and guarded her soul on its flight. And some said they saw two strangers, one on either side of her, though their clothes never burned, and they shone like the sun. So weep not, my love. Thy mother was no witch. I know that now, with all my heart."

"Why did she have to die, then?"

"Because men are not always wise and make mistakes."

Leonard lifted his head and searched his father's face. "She died like a queen?" he asked earnestly.

"Yea, right bravely."

The boy smiled, his face radiant. And Edmund gathered up his son and hugged him close, and carried him along the path between the trees, in and out of the pools of sunlight, and past the tall yellow-flowering plants of the herb of grace.

Author's Note

What Juniper and Dylan did through meditation and visualization was in no way connected with séances, contacting spirits of the dead, hypnotism, or reincarnation. *The Juniper Game* is about memory-like experiences and contains what I believe to be a truth — that there is no time as we measure it.

About the Author

Sherryl Jordan is a full-time author who enjoys reading and listening to music. Of her writing she says, "I hope through my books to bring young people something that is positive, uplifting, and joyful."

Ms. Jordan lives in Tauranga, New Zealand, with her husband Lee, and their daughter Kym.